On My Aunt's
Shallow Grave
White Roses
Have Already
Bloomed

On My Aunt's Shallow Grave White Roses Have Already Bloomed

Maria Mitsora

Translated from the Greek by Jacob Moe

Yale UNIVERSITY PRESS · NEW HAVEN AND LONDON

A MARGELLOS
WORLD REPUBLIC OF LETTERS BOOK

The Margellos World Republic of Letters is dedicated to making literary works from around the globe available in English through translation. It brings to the English-speaking world the work of leading poets, novelists, essayists, philosophers, and playwrights from Europe, Latin America, Africa, Asia, and the Middle East to stimulate international discourse and creative exchange.

Yale University Press books may be purchased in quantity for educational, business, or promotional use. For information, please e-mail sales.press@ yale.edu (U.S. office) or sales@yaleup.co.uk (U.K. office).

Set in Baskerville MT and Nobel types by Tseng Information Systems, Inc., Durham, North Carolina. Printed in the United States of America.

Library of Congress Control Number: 2018933286
ISBN 978-0-300-21576-2 (paper : alk. paper)

A catalogue record for this book is available from the British Library.

This paper meets the requirements of ANSI/NISO z39.48–1992 (Permanence of Paper).

10 9 8 7 6 5 4 3 2 1

Contents

Translator's Preface

When I first embarked on this translation, Maria Mitsora handed me a copy of the book with a scrawled dedication borrowed from the blues guitarist Walter "Furry" Lewis: "I've got a new way of spelling Memphis, Tennessee." Right below, she added, "and a new way of spelling Athens, Greece." The phrase acknowledged both the book's precise attention to language and its unrelentingly playful bid to reinvent it. With this blues refrain in mind, I began re-spelling *On My Aunt's Shallow Grave White Roses Have Already Bloomed* into English, surrounded in my imagination by the contents of Mitsora's apartment—scattered blues LPs, a plaster bust of Mercury, a yellowing stack of detective novels and dictionaries, a paperback copy of Jorge Luis Borges's collected short stories—a patchwork of objects and texts progressively woven into Mitsora's writing over the course of four decades.

Before her first collection of short stories, *Anna, Here's Another One* ['Άννα, να ένα άλλο], appeared in 1978, Mitsora had published work in *Kouros,* an underground literary magazine described by a younger writer, Giorgos-Ikaros Babasakis, as where he "learned the secret history of the twentieth century." Other magazines, such as *Tram* and *Chroniko,* to which Mitsora also contributed, served as both venues for a new generation of countercurrent Greek writers and places to become acquainted with foreign literary movements in Greek translation, particularly from the Americas and western Europe— the Beat Generation, OULIPO, and magical realism, among others. It was these movements that exerted a decisive influence on the forms and themes of Mitsora's own work.

Her subsequent books—four novels, a novella, and two collections of short stories— explore the alternatingly dark and revelatory vagaries of the human psyche, depicting a world in which her protagonists are caught between reality and myth, predestination and chance, rationality and twisted dreams. Alexandra, the heroine of the novel *Diffuse Power* [*Σκόρπια Δύναμη*] (1982), wanders through a largely abandoned Athens, encountering a city bleaker and more corrupt than the few characters she meets along the way as the physical landscape and the space of the mind intersect in this urban netherworld of the 1980s. A later novel, *Fair Weather/ Movement* [*Καλός καιρός/Μετακίνηση*] (2005), remains an outlier in its realist style and unequivocally rhapsodic view of love and human relationships: Alkis, a young editor, moves in two floors down from Elli, a married housewife, and they subsequently engage in a blissful affair that lacks the dire fatalism in which many of her previous characters seem trapped. *My Name's Word* [*Με λένε λέξη*] (2008), an autobiographical narrative of sorts, sends us "sailing on the froth of words, looking for the way back toward that first emotion linking us to people and things."

To introduce the reader to the range of Mi-

tsora's work, *On My Aunt's Shallow Grave White
Roses Have Already Bloomed* assembles sixteen of
her short stories. With the exception of an addi-
tional story, "The Silkworm's Address," it contains the same stories found in the Greek collection published under the name *From the Waist
Down* [Από τη μέση και κάτω] in October 2014. Nine
stories were published in Greek newspapers and
magazines over the past thirty years and revised
extensively by the author for that publication;
the other six were completely new. In offering
a survey of the predominant styles and themes
of Mitsora's writing, this collection sketches a
trajectory from earlier, restless experiments to
later, more resolute narratives. The most recent
story in the collection, written in 2015, finds salvation in the act of writing itself when "T.," a
former lover, urges the narrator to take her own
life: "Sometimes on the morning of New Year's
Day his voice still dares me, 'Don't waste away
your time with a slow death.' Hastily, I take up
pen and paper to fill the gaping mouth of Time
with words."

These stories engage a wide spectrum of real and imagined intertexts: professed literary influences, formative experiences in the Athenian underground scene, objects, phrases, and songs reaching from China to Amman and Justa Fé—an invented Latin American town to which the narrator of "Zenaida Junona" seeks to return, only to learn that it no longer exists. Science fiction, most present in "Dogwise" and "Althea's Prophecy," coexists with magical realism and realism throughout the collection, embodying an irreverence to genre common in Greek literary history. This heterogeneous, international range enables a direct conversation with the literary resources of the English language. Equally comfortable with street slang, biblical language, and neologism, Mitsora's prose contains nods to Poe's fascination with the macabre, Faulknerian stream of consciousness, and the sonority of Molly Bloom's soliloquy in *Ulysses*—which Mitsora herself insists must be read aloud. Attentive portraits of the female subconscious bring to mind work by Katherine Mansfield and Flannery O'Connor. Other, more recent points of reference include Robert Coover's fragmented narratives, Mary Gaitskill's marginal characters, and Margaret Atwood's dystopian visions of the future.

We should go a step farther than these Anglophone influences in reading this collection; *On My Aunt's Shallow Grave White Roses Have Already Bloomed* also fills a gap in the increasing corpus of modern Greek literature now available in the English language. Recent translations (and re-translations) of seminal contemporary work allow Mitsora's stories to enter into conversation with preceding and contemporary authors, sketching a rich and representative panorama. Most immediately, we can look to the diverse works already included in the Margellos World Republic of Letters series, to recent short story collections by authors such as Christos Ikonomou, and to the new multilingual Greek poetry included in the anthology *Austerity Measures* published by Penguin in 2016.

In a world where literature in translation accounts for less than 2–4 percent of work published in English, we can consider reading translations as a political act: a way of counteracting dominant forms of cultural exchange, and engaging cultural and literary traditions different from our own. Yet there is also a sense in which these stories come from a familiar place at a familiar moment. Mitsora's generation emerged just as Greece began to heal from the forces of excessive nationalism and political polarization. Today, as the xenophobic Golden Dawn Party remains a force to contend with in the Greek Parliament, and anti-globalization attitudes propel formerly marginal candidates to prominence, it is instructive to revisit Mitsora's inventive havens of personal resistance and to understand her work as both a product of a newly relevant historical moment and a nod to the affirming possibilities of human imagination.

These stories, whether set underground, lodged deep in the subconscious, or scattered across Latin America, share a keen and playful border with our everyday, lived worlds. In "The

End of the Show," the collection's last story, the narrator makes an attempt to kill a persistently buzzing wasp, spraying it with insecticide through the screen door. Although "darkness swallow[s] the end of the show," the yellow jacket buzzes into the distance and out of frame. In a recent email, Mitsora quipped: "Yesterday I was stung by a yellow jacket as I was picking figs, my arm swelled up all the way to my elbow. Could it have been a distant cousin of the one I doused?" This thin interface between fiction and reality, this precarious relation between cause and effect is shared by her protagonists and their adventures in the following pages. Mitsora's world is such that it lets readers believe that a spiteful act of fiction might just be avenged in real life, and that the end is, well, never quite the end.

On My Aunt's
Shallow Grave
White Roses
Have Already
Bloomed

For L, forever daring me to take a leap into the stormy sea of August

Thanks

Thanks to Yanna Boufi for her help, for the advice, and for the fun too.

Introduction: The Bee Is on the Tree

Falling in love with a language can be as overwhelming as falling in love with a person. I started learning English at the age of seven. My tutor lived in a beautiful pink-stone house, enveloped in bougainvillea vines. I had heard a few things about his life story; I knew that his English wife had dropped dead descending the stairs during an evening ball. There was a back garden growing wildly, used as headquarters by a gang of crows. I never caught a glimpse of the rest of the house; I only ever got to see his study with its wall-length bookcases and wood-burning stove.

I fell in love with the English language by the glow of the fire, feeling the presence of a ghost in a long white gown, hearing the panicky noise made by the wings of a bird which once got caught in the stove's metal pipes. Maybe I was also influenced by an expression I learned: "A murder of crows." A lifetime later I wrote a short story inspired by this experience, called "The Pythagorean Birds," in which the birds' patterns of flight traced equations of death in the air. The first sentence I memorized in English was "The bee is on the tree."

Years later I fell in love with French, with its flowery syntax, its tongue-bending pronunciation. Unfaithful to English, I even married a Frenchman, devouring French literature. I never tried to acquire a perfect accent in any language though, knowing that sooner or later I would be caught in disguise. The first sentence I memorized was "Au clair de la lune, mon ami Pierrot, prête-moi ta plume pour écrire un mot." (Under the moonlight, Pierrot my friend, lend me your pen so I may write a note.) Already, a hint about writing.

As I was getting divorced from Paul-François, I started studying German. The very first sentence still comes to mind: "Dem Bahnhof gegenüber stehen zwei Hotels." (There are two hotels opposite the train station.) I guess by then I was in a hurry to live my life and could not be delayed any longer by going back to my Ancient Greek grammar books for a better understanding of German syntax. Besides, this sentence had the railway in it, along with the departing trains, so I abandoned German after a year. By that time I had started to realize my fate: I would have to live in Athens, hostage of the Greek language . . .

Years passed before I stood outside the Museo del Oro, in Santa Fe de Bogotá. On its walls I read the inscription of the Kogui text about the origins of the world, the sea being both prophesy and memory. I had already fallen passionately in love with a new language. Despite many escapades in Latin America, the prophecy behind the first remembered Spanish phrase, "porque mi novio es argentino" (because my fiancé is from Argentina), was never realized.

Mallarmé's line "a throw of the dice will never abolish chance" was still hanging above my head like a moon when I considered the present translation, new words picking different locks, breaking and entering. I asked the *Book of Changes* (I Ching) for advice; its answer was "it furthers one to cross the great water . . . though he steps on the tail of the tiger. Good fortune, when done playfully." Since many characters in my books playfully pull at Cerberus's tail, I decided to take the risk with the tiger's tail, too.

I often have the feeling that the stories I have written do not belong to me; in my mind, the dance had always prevailed over the dancer. Certainly, they are the result of my time/space and character. According to Heraclitus's famous quote, "ἦθος ἀνθρώπῳ δαίμων," our character is our daimon, eventually our destiny. In any case, both reading and writing remind me of the lyrics from an old Van Morrison song: "To be born again in another place, in another face." Not only as a wish but also as an invitation to role play—highly pleasurable, redeeming, sometimes therapeutic too.

The Cat That Can't Dance

For Rena Bistika

Each day I am a different creature of God. In the eyes of others I am human, a man. Oh boy, how that makes me laugh. Thirty-three years old, like Alexander the Great, like Jesus. Yesterday, my light feet led me once again to the café where she often sits drinking hot chocolate with her friend. Her friend has a joyful black-and-white dog. I think its name is Liebe, German for "love." They have a few smartly dressed guys for company, who tell jokes and laugh loudly. My love lowers her head modestly, her red hair falling over her face like a velvet curtain at the end of the show. From the bench where I sit disguised, sometimes as a lottery ticket vendor, sometimes as a street musician, I can only see half her smile. This is my sadness, this is my salvation, since if it ever hit me full on, I would have been love-struck on the spot, incapable of getting back to my house and my cat Snow White. Yesterday I was a snail, and I managed to return by following the thin silver trail I had left on the asphalt. Last Friday her friend's dog was barking at me, as I, a black pigeon, fluttered over their table, raising a gust of wind with my wings, wrapping her in my savage spirit . . .

At times I wish I could get to the beginning of my story. But the beginning is lost in darkness, even more than the end. Until now, I've just been one of the strangers in the square, though I hope she will soon realize that each moment I lay eyes on her time freezes, an assembly of demons cunningly, deceitfully seeking to push me off-balance. They even spark love affairs among those around me, premised on the victory of evil over good. My mouth dries at the very thought of her, and my forlorn tower of morality crumbles as my desire rushes irrepressibly, ruthlessly toward her.

How I wish I could get back to the beginning . . . As a child, I was very quiet, very absentminded. I liked books about travel, maps, and documentaries showing far-away places. I was also very fond of *Alice in Wonderland*. Reading through its pages, I realized that miracles were not necessarily benevolent, or, in any case, that wonders differed from wonderful things. I never knew my parents. I was raised by a distant aunt who had been widowed twice, first by a ship captain, then by a cloth merchant. She was a cheery woman without meaning the least bit well. I do not recall, however, that she made any offensive remarks about my parents abandoning me. She knew nothing about my father, and avoided talking about my mother, who had embarked on an ocean liner to pursue her career as a singer in Argentina straight out of the maternity ward. I do know that her hair was red. Every Christmas my aunt would set up a nice pine tree, piled with delicate antique ornaments and topped with a slightly crooked, colorful star. Of all the glittering little balls my favorite was the dullest, a pink one, dented, neither round nor oval. I have only one photograph of my mother, wearing an evening gown and holding a microphone to her lips before a table of men—but ha! Now it comes to me that this odd little pink ball might have reminded me of her breast. That's probably why it was my first heartless love. When I turned twelve, my aunt gave the tree with all its ornaments to the church program for refugee aid. Around that time, something inside me changed. I overcame my fear of God, and this gave me a feeling of immeasurable strength. I would lock myself in the bathroom and paint my body in war colors with my aunt's lipstick. Whenever she found me out, she would punish me severely. She forced me to wear tight shoes under the pretense of cutting costs. One thing is certain: though I grew to be five foot ten, I wear size six shoes. Nowadays I buy bigger ones and stuff them with tissue paper. Will the red-haired girl laugh at the sight of my bare feet? Will she scorn me like the members of the committee for exemption from military service? As I grew up I became quite nasty, torturing my aunt's dog, that old servile, sycophantic Judas. Anyway, what does it matter what I was back then?

What really matters is that at some point I swore to kill my aunt for never loving me, for never giving me the chance to become good.

But I was scared of jail, and that's the only reason I was consumed by a flame of revenge for over twenty years. Bit by bit our neighborhood changed. Anonymity spread here as well, the familiar faces gone. So, when the time came, the act of killing her was devoid of any emotion. As she grew old, I took care of her out of habit, as if she were a broken doll. Her chronic cough and that pathetic gratitude in her eyes whenever I massaged her cold feet were getting on my nerves. She was a seventy-eight-year-old wreck, in constant pain from arthritis. I'm not trying to impress anybody with my little crime; I only pressed the pillow down on her face. She didn't even fight back, she just dug into the pillowcase with her nails. This lack of a struggle, the absence of any violence at all, made me feel that I had committed a nearly beneficial murder with the consent of both victim and perpetrator—and this made me feel emptier than ever. I washed her, dressed her in her favorite gown, then buried her in the garden with a vague feeling of sadness. Afterward, I remember eating a rice pudding. Outside a Gypsy in his truck kept shouting that he was buying scrap metal and old television sets, but I sure knew he wasn't buying old hags.

This happened two years ago, in the month of August, and last year it was August again when I found Snow White, my cat . . . a dirty ball of fluff being kicked around by some monstrous kids. I managed to snatch her from them and left, running, as she curled up in my armpit. After I washed her and cleaned her ears with cotton swabs, she transformed into an astonishingly beautiful white dwarf cat, never growing past her size at six months. Snow White's shiny coat aired out most of the darkness in my life, and soon I had the feeling that Rita's hair would grace my garden with its shades of red.

Her red mane captivated me first. That's when I knew she was my Aphrodite, destined to fit my pockets. I want her skin as lining for my overcoat, I yearn to drink her blue eyes out of a glass, to have her lips sewn. Quietly, oh so quietly, without a single word, I want her to teach me how to dance. A chilling desire runs down my spine and the memory of her beauty torments me, the memory of her slight silhouette as she disappears into her house. An inner voice commands me to keep stalking her in disguise. Cursed animal, it whispers, you must lure the pale red-haired girl to your garden.

My garden is small, wedged between two apartment buildings. I emerge from the kitchen holding a cup full of Indian nut milk. I sit with my back to the house, enclosed within tall bare walls, left and right. I have fastened thick bamboo mats along the fence so that I am invisible to the street, so that no one can tell whether I am sitting naked or wearing my long coat. In this little kingdom of mine there is a carob tree and an aging jasmine, blossoming madly as it tries to invade the house. The white roses I planted last year on my aunt's grave have already bloomed. When Rita comes, we will plant daisy seeds. Because her name is Rita, short for Margarita— the Greek word for daisy. Did I guess it, overhear it, invent it? I wonder where she might be this very moment, but the noises from the street distract me. Cars and mopeds pass through my head as they chug fitfully up an imaginary hill. I will myself to a white landscape where sleds glide on the horizon, the whistle of an invisible riverboat signaling a scheduled departure. I bring the cup to my lips; it is Indian nut milk, yet it isn't—now it has acquired the exact consistency of semen. Snow White comes and rubs at my feet, it is her purring that brings me back to the present. Sometimes when the full moon overflows, she dances on the grave of my good old aunt, who took me in and cared for me before she became a ghost. Snow White tries to lift my spirits but I drag my feet, since I am the cat that can't dance. Snow White, pray for me to the god of the deserts and deserted souls. After I bathed you and dried you, you transformed into a princess. Rita, if that is indeed her name, what will she transform me into? This Rita, if I pluck her, will she tell me she loves me not?

I laugh to myself, and that is no good. Yesterday at the flea market heads turned after me as I walked past, smiling, pleased with the perfection of my disguise. A gray banker's suit, a balding head, a fat tummy, and a tie with gentle, well-meaning stripes. But perhaps I would have made less of an impression with my real face? The symmetry of my features is comforting. My fine manners betray a well-educated individual with the composure of a superior mammal. I have a straight nose, straight brow, and light blue eyes like hers. An old man I helped across the street told me, "Thank you, son." Only strangers have ever called me that, and it feels so bittersweet. Over the years wandering through flea markets, I have collected thirty-two tiny porcelain frogs, half of them crowned, the other half crownless. I keep them lined up in two rows on the oval dining room table.

It is Monday, and I've woken up with the premonition that I won't see her. Tuesdays and Thursdays I follow her downtown to the Cervantes Institute, across from the cathedral. Pray for me, Snow White, because today I am in mourning; it is the anniversary of my dear aunt's death. I awoke at the first light of dawn to bury her pearl necklace in the garden, but the dawn fooled me. Now the shutter of her bedroom window is banging over and over again and the world is chiding me for my cowardice. I burst out in anger, swearing that if I see Rita I'll invite her to my garden, revealing my true face, using a real cat as bait.

I have a dim recollection of how it happened. Snow White immediately grasped my plan and grinned behind her whiskers as I placed her in her basket. Rita recognized me at once, most likely from the pharmacy. She came closer to get a better look at the cat, asking to pet it. To me, each beginning is even more mysterious than the end. But it was relatively easy to strike up a conversation, more so because this wasn't the beginning, this was halfway to the end. Her name was Rita, indeed, nineteen years old, and she wanted to become a beautician to make the world prettier. My ears buzzed. *What are you? What are you?* I wanted to scream at her. *Looking deep into me with your tranquil eyes, will you see some worth in me?* We walked together to my house and sat in the garden, Snow White almost immediately settling in her lap. "I have two brothers," I heard her say, while I wished she would take me across to the shores of an unambiguous world. With mannered charm, she held the fine saucer from my aunt's good tea service set. It was as simple as that; she started coming to my garden every afternoon. Could she be a treacherous sprite, a demon? To soothe my inner turmoil I kept telling her of distant places, for instance, the San Blas archipelago outside Panama City. Each time she walked out of the house I wondered whether she left a trail of evil in her wake.

"Have you really seen rivers the color of tea?" The interest in her eyes dwindled when I said that I had not. I kept talking to her just so she would not ask me to go inside the house again, dreading the furniture that knew me through and through.

"Do you know how to dance?" I asked, my face turning red hot.

"I know how to salsa; I'm learning Spanish because I want to go to Cuba with the first money I make on my own." *Looks like all you young girls want to go to Cuba these days,* I felt like saying.

"But we have the cat," I whispered. She heard it and smiled. She had beautiful teeth, not sharp at all, nearly rounded at the edges like daisy petals. Her smile had the power to infuriate me at times. I could have backhanded her. Could I? And this is how the second week of September passed, Rita coming to my house in the early evening, I welcoming her with pastries, both of us going to sit in the garden.

"I am still trying to figure you out": each of her words a slap in the face.

"To figure out what?" To figure out why I looked at her only from the neck up?

"I saw you in my sleep last night; it was you but it wasn't you, somehow you were a tangled ball of yarns."

"Cotton or wool?" I mumbled, just to say something, as she wet her lips with her tongue.

"I don't know, probably a bit of both."

"And what did you do with the yarns? Were they knotted up?"

"I was looking inside a suitcase for knitting needles. I wanted to make a nice sweater to wear over my bare skin." Could it be time to propose to her?

"Your friend's dog is called Liebe?"

"No, Libby, for 'liberty.'"

I sighed unintentionally. "I have never felt free," I stammered.

"Free from what?"

"Good question, good question," I said, looking to gain some time.

Were those afternoons we spent together meaningful? I still couldn't make up my mind. All the same, she had a strong sense of intuition, that much I admit. As she glanced at the roses over my aunt's grave, she remarked that the loveliest grow in cemeteries.

"Why don't you show me around the house?" She was pressing me again. "You have so many beautiful things."

"The house oppresses me. Before I met you I spent most of my time in the garden. Even in the rain, I'd sit under a large umbrella, closing my eyes at times, trying to imagine I was on a boat crossing all the lakes with sunken villages in their depths." She took in my knowledge of geography admiringly.

"You will teach me geography and I will teach you how to dance." I shivered, my armpits dripping milk and honey. Could she be so naive?

"What size shoes do you wear?" I asked, in a slip of the tongue.

"Six. You've got small feet for your height, small feet but large hands." I felt a new abyss gaping in front of me, beneath the already familiar one. But she clapped her hands at one of Snow White's pirouettes, and miraculously we were both saved.

Snow White would often nestle on her lap, winking at me. If they formed a true alliance, these two female creatures could rip me apart, limb from limb. I had to find out if she ever talked to others about her visits, if she spilled the details: an old two-story house, squeezed between two apartment buildings, a garden hidden completely from view. Maybe she had even given away my full address. She startled me once more. This time I was convinced she had special gifts. Easily disarming me with her innocent looks, she could read my thoughts. My garden was in danger as she answered before I could utter the question, her eyes fixed on my stuffed sneakers. "No, I have not spoken a word to anyone." I asked myself whether she could see through to my deformed toes.

"What am I thinking? Take a guess."

"I can't, not right this moment." She didn't sound as if she were lying. "It's tough to guess because you're like a child, your mind full of hidden rooms, unformed thoughts. That's what I like about you, you are so different." She tried to muddy the waters as she deciphered me.

"You haven't talked about me to your friends? Not even to your friend's dog, Libby?" She flashed that wonderful smile of hers again, now a trifle maternal, and I saw her eyelashes moist with tiny diamonds. To be precise, she blinked and teared up the moment I was ready to scream, "Don't stare at me like that, as if you'd given birth to me!"

"I'd never tell anybody anything. This garden belongs only to you and Snow White, and maybe just a tiny bit to me too." She sprang up and left in a near sprint, leaving me close to tears and loathing her for it.

Margarita did not show up the next day, nor in the days to come. No more coffee in the square; she was skipping Spanish class too. Dressed as a town hall employee, I rang her doorbell. The woman who answered the door was the owner of the pharmacy where Margarita often helped with the cosmetics section. At last I was sure it was her mother. Was she notified with regard to the rats in the sewers, I asked.

"No, no," she shuddered, and then stepped out, locking the door behind her. I followed her at a distance until she got into a cab. For a whole week Snow White was lost in grief while I sought out the busy streets, staying away from the house for hours at a time, though not before bidding her farewell with a tip of my hat.

Time passed torturously with the certainty she was shedding her clothes elsewhere. December arrived, its lonely holidays a frightening prospect ever since my pink ball had been lost for good. I kept trying to stay out of the house, taking the train down to the port of Piraeus, walking up to the docks where the big ships moored, looking for those that might carry secret cargoes of faraway landscapes. *My life is a fairy tale,* I kept thinking, and I could hear the voice of an old storyteller, "Theeere he is," the voice would say, "He hits the road again all by his lonesome self . . ." Then one morning I awoke terrified that I had become transparent, my evil thoughts and deeds glowing for all to see. I sat in the garden, now stripped of all its kindness.

When the hard rains arrived I had already settled under my umbrella in the garden, the buzz of the empty fridge reaching my ears like the battle preparations of an army of flies. Snow

White had lost her wits, avoiding me, sleeping on my aunt's bed upstairs. It was December 20, probably the last day of my life. *What would become of Snow White?* I worried. She couldn't end up back on the street. Then I thought of setting a stool directly below the crawl space in the bathroom, building a small gallows. Thankfully, death didn't frighten me. I brought my aunt's sleeping pills downstairs, placing them in a kitchen drawer stuffed with her embroidered coasters.

I was sitting awkwardly, a visitor, in the big armchair in the living room. The doorbell rang, softly at first. By the time it rang again I was a stranger in my own body. I walked to the door, dragging my feet. Rita stood there, more pale, more beautiful than ever, holding a box of sweets and a red balloon. Something about her had changed. The same lips, the same long eyelashes, but in her face an irrational emotion.

"Forgive me," she whispered, and fell into my embrace. That is, she fell into the void without realizing it, as I hastily put my arms around her shoulders.

"I've been in England because my brother had some serious health problems," she said into my ear. I remained unmoved, rock solid, even though she had ruined my life. Without looking around she passed me, entered the living room and dropped straight into my armchair. I pulled up the ottoman I used to prop my aunt's feet on whenever I gave her a pedicure.

"What's wrong with you? What's up?" Rita was addressing me. I must have been eyeing her strangely. "Rita" was all I could utter, while thinking, "nevermore, Margarita."

"I went to London on the outside chance that my brother had lymph cancer. I never mentioned it because I only wanted to bring joy to your garden. Look, I brought some cheesecake," she tried to calm me with her lighthearted tone, rising and placing the box of sweets on the tabletop. As she noticed the collection of little frogs I heard her exclaim, "Oh, how sweet, the crowned ones and the grieving ones in two different rows."

I retrieved my steady voice. "Let's go to the garden, it isn't cold, it's just a bit muddy, and anyways, the fridge has gotten too chatty in here."

With the balloon still in hand, she opened the door and called, "Let's eat the sweets, bring them out." Behind her back, I took a quick glance inside the drawer with the sleeping pills, stealthily shutting it again. Holding the tray, I stepped on a snail and Rita, sitting on the wicker chair, burst into tears.

"Why? Why? It had its little life too." Deathly shadows played hide-and-seek with the pale evening light in my garden as the beautiful, silly girl praised the world's many wonders. Snow White picked that moment to jump into her lap.

"Snow White, my darling, you look prettier than ever," Rita said with a teary smile. Then, I don't know what possessed me, I decided to tell her everything, in the faint voice of a ghost. I told her about my aunt, about my aunt's shallow grave, about my mother whose name was also Margarita, who had red hair too. At first she scrutinized me with a scientific curiosity, and at the very moment I expected terror in her eyes, the balloon she let go of nearly caught on the carob tree. Pointing at its upward flight, she said to me:

"That's how sadness fades away; it returns to the sky. Your aunt is already lighter than air. I've read a lot of detective stories, and I've come to the conclusion that sometimes murderers are like children who never grew up." I sat there speechless, wondering how on earth I came across her. This one is able to teach me how to dance.

From the
Waist Down

Would I fall to my knees for a single perfect sentence? Inhaling inquisitively, exhaling in wonder, I await the revelation. Yesterday I was reading the story of Houadjia Hassan El Habal, the poorest of the poor, whose whole life's savings amounted to a piece of lead. His neighbor, the fisherman, needed the piece to weigh down his nets, and when he granted it to him willingly, Houadjia was promised the first catch from the big river. But when the nets were cast, the fisherman caught a singular fish, an inch wide and as long as a forearm. No matter whether he kept casting the nets again and again, whether he pulled them out full to the brim—Houadjia Hassan El Habal was only due that first fish. He accepted it, singing praises to God, and then gave it to his wife, who was dumbfounded at the sight. She began scaling it in the kitchen, splitting its belly, whereupon a precious stone slipped out, so large and brilliant that it lit the room for the entire night. In what dark, icy waters does my fish swim? Or perhaps it hides from me at the bottom of an emerald lake? It darts and hides between sharp rocks, darting and shivering at its fate. For I am its fate, and every road leads to me. I've even caught a glimpse of its tail in a ditch of rainwater. I have neither hook nor knife, but even if I could grasp it with my bare hands, as soon as I felt it wriggle, I'd throw it back in the water. Nor could I crush it with my hands upon the rocks. I am strangely unable to grind it into a pulp, turning its agony into diamonds, its suffocating gasps into a gentle wind that could narrate my story, blowing the words back and forth between the lines of my manuscript. The story of someone who cannot kill with his own hands, so he keeps killing the same woman over and over again with his thoughts.

He has a dream. A black iron bridge links the two banks of a river, making a strange loop in the air. High up there he stands with his beloved. She is a mermaid now. Repulsed by her scales, he looks in wonder at the butcher shops lining the shore. Their large inscriptions proclaim all types of meat: tiger, deer, lion, snake, antelope. Vehicles stop and human figures hurriedly fill the trunks, while a line of cars behind them honk impatiently. All the lights, weak and strong, cast a funereal shade of purple. He feels a deep desperation. Leaning over her his mind races, embracing her before his hands can reach her. He smells her even before he nestles his nose in her flowing hair. But she is utterly unfamiliar now; even her throat tastes like charcoal, and his nostrils speak, telling him, *Smells like human meat.* His senses hate her, driving his hands to beat her mercilessly until she is lying limp at his feet, her jaw slack, the dimple in her chin he was so crazy about filled with a drop of blood. He pulls her up, unsure of how to get rid of her. One of the butcher shops, he ponders, might take her for human meat—at least from the waist up. He descends the stairs carrying her body in his arms, her weight decreasing with each step, whatever remains of her becoming more precious by the second.

The bells of hell ring in unison. Abandoning the inanimate mermaid on the threshold of sleep, he pulls the blanket off his head. Outside the window the sky is still dark. The bell keeps ringing. He opens the door to see Vicky flickering in the hallway's low light . . . Both of them stand speechless in the kitchen while he makes coffee. "He hit me," mumbles Vicky, and he's sure he misheard—now she will tell him, "You beat me up but you didn't kill me, that's why I'm here"—yet people only share the same dreams in fairy tales. Vicky, supporting herself on the kitchen table, eyes fixed on the spice rack, speaks loud and clear this time. "He heard me call your name in my sleep, I told him about us and he hit me." At last he understands. For over a year and a half he has hated her for not leaving her husband. Now she has finally come to his house to live with him. Still dazed, he double-locks his half-finished novel in the office desk drawer.

For the next ten days Vicky wears his clothes, cleans the house, and cooks fish. In the dark drawer, the unfinished novel is secretly protesting. But in the bedroom he still hopes to discover Houadjia Hassan El Habal's gem deep inside her belly. And then, on the eleventh day, returning home late from work, "Surprise!" she says, as she opens the front door. She is wearing a skintight black dress, an orange shawl draped around her shoulders. Her clothes and shoes are scattered all around the living room. "Let's get out of here and celebrate! I knew he'd be away from Athens today, so I got into the house and took my things." The surprise lies elsewhere— next to the desk where he keeps his manuscript locked, she has installed an illuminated aquarium. A black fish with an orange mane swims through the transparent water. "I can't believe he kept feeding it," says Vicky; "can't believe I found it alive. He had killed the last one with scalding water in a fit of jealousy . . . Sometimes the future spills into the present. Before we met I had already secretly baptized this one with your name." Mesmerized he watches his namesake crawling out from between two sharp rocks, opening and closing its mouth, producing unintelligible bubbles. What perfect sentence could it be dictating? Vicky's voice stirs up waves that muddle his thoughts, asking again and again which pair of shoes she should wear. She's in a rush to go out dancing. The fish disappears into the seaweed. Fate, the blind goddess, has tricked him. The novel will remain unfinished. Madness, sometimes, breaks suddenly into the room.

Downtown Athens

A love affair in the underworld

J ohn liked his very common name. He felt it set him free to dwell on the wildest thoughts. Now, dressed as Santa Claus, standing in the middle of the square by the city hall as he was giving balloons out to children, supplementing the little money he made teaching math classes, he idly thought, to pass the time . . . *I should've become a painter, sculptor, or plastic surgeon. Or rather a muralist, decorating rooftops held captive between sky-high buildings with scenes of flawless perspective and fountains flowing down to the pavement with all the flavors of melting ice cream. For you, kids!*

"Here, you take a red balloon, you take a green . . ." *On those towering walls I would draw golden rays heavy as chains, piercing leaden clouds, proving the existence of an inferior, evil deity constantly inventing international crises. Yep, one somersault for Santa, another one for John, and here, kiddos, take some more balloons . . .* He glanced at the time and at the clearing sky, and when his gaze dropped back down he saw her approaching. Long-limbed, with

golden-brown hair, she wore a glossy black raincoat, her measured stride, long neck, and loose
braid immediately reminding him of a caryatid.

He stood inside the circle of children. When
their eyes locked, John felt a strange flutter and
winked involuntarily. Embarrassed by his own
reaction, he began giving out more balloons.
When his eyes cut up to hers again, he was
thrilled by the feeling that her dark gaze had
draped him in a magic cloak. As a kid he'd heard
someone say that women were mystery trains,
and, taking the phrase literally, tried to imagine
the strange lands they would carry you through
if they ever gripped you in their naked embrace.
Later, in his first adolescent daydreams, he kept
wondering how it would feel to be held between
their thighs. Could it be that he'd discover an
icy landscape strewn with gravestones, or some-
where in the depths a scorching sky? Well, none
of this happened. It was sweet and warm, devoid of ecstasy. But why remember all this now?
Because her eyes shone like the caverns of a dia-
mond mine. He saw her stepping backward and

was terrified that she'd leave and disappear for good. Turning away from his little audience, he scribbled something on his cigarette pack and made his way through the crowd to give it to her. The girl read, "In front of Krinos on Aeolou Street in forty minutes." Holding the pack by the tips of her fingers, she walked away and turned the corner.

John got to Krinos in forty minutes exactly. He had his own clothes on, though the red cap was still perched on his head. She stood by the entrance, the smell of pancakes and honey wafting out.

"My name's John."

"Mine's Joan," she said, both of them laughing. "First time I've had Santa Claus wink at me."

"When did you stop believing he existed?"

"When I was very young. After they read me 'The Little Match Girl,' Andersen's fairy tale. I guess because it taught me that the same day a birth is celebrated, others are dying of hunger or cold."

"Shall we go inside? Don't you want to sit down?" John wanted to keep on asking questions just to hear her voice.

"No," she said, almost alarmed, "Please, I'd rather walk." *Good thing she's wearing flats*, thought John, *because women in heels snub the ground they walk on.*

They strolled down Evripidou Street, with its smells of spices, and anyone catching sight of them would think they were two beautiful siblings or a couple madly in love, looking for a night's shelter in the dark side streets of the city center. But if an astronomer were to notice them, he'd exclaim, "Hey, how strange. Two unknown stars promenading together throughout the universe."

They arrived at the Monastiraki market, walking silently by the train tracks. At the beginning of Agiou Pavlou Street, the splendid new moon stopped them short for a second, its cold light shining warmly just for them. At the peddlers' sidewalk benches, John dawdled to take a look. In the end he picked out a pair of luminous green earrings with a merry Chinese dragon engraved in the center. As they passed by the sidewalk cafés opposite Theseus's temple, Joan timidly put them on. They'd taken Akamantos Street and began climbing to the road encircling Filopappou Park. Then railings halted them, and for a moment Joan looked worriedly at the dark mass of trees.

"Don't be afraid, I just want to show you a splendid view."

Like elves, they slid into the fenced-off space. Joan gasped at the sight of the two white horses bathed in the moon's cold white light, shining warmly just for them. "They're from the last horse-drawn carriage in Athens," explained John, "they still rent it out for weddings." Climbing farther up the hill, they breathed in the silent sleep of the pines, the eucalyptus, and the cypress trees. Suddenly, from within a cluster of immortal cacti, they saw the planetarium's metallic cap at their feet, transforming the twilight to a celebration. Behind them, on the horizon, they guessed at the expanse of the sea. The

Acropolis stood front and center, beyond it the hills and mountains of Lycabettus and Hymettos. On the other side Mount Penteli, and still farther the ridge of Egaleo, where Xerxes had once watched his defeat in the naval battle of Salamis.[1]

"My grandmother was religious. I can recite the end of the Apocalypse of Saint John to you by memory," said Joan, rapt.

"So can I," he whispered, ecstatic. "I create a new heaven and a new earth, behold! The new holy city of Athens descending from heaven adorned."[2] He embraced her and kissed her on the mouth passionately. Above them baby bats tested their patterns of nocturnal flight, as a single ray of moonlight was explaining to her sisters that she had urgent work in this underworld, on earth, to tightly bond this young couple, a kouros and kore, uniting them forever, innocent and well-fated through time.

The Suzani and
the Scooter

On an overnight ferry, nestled in a cabin with hospital hues, I selected the words: *shorts, sardines, pine needles, suzani, scooter, deserted,* and a burning future.

She approached him abruptly, breaking into his secret circle. "I've had a vision," she said, raising her head, her expression dead serious; "you'll have a tattoo done right here." With her index finger she touched the dimple of his thigh under the pelvic bone through his baggy shorts. "A black butterfly never in flight, constantly reposing."

She flew away from him and started running. She was a born runner, very young, barely sixteen, comprehending it all through running. At first she wondered why the boy—working at his father's café on the white beach where the pleasure boats docked—tried to keep up with her and her torn jeans. Dazed by her silhouette, he couldn't tear his eyes off her as she ran along in front of him on the island's narrowest point. She looked like a twelve-year-old boy, very short black hair, broad shoulders, winged feet, invisible azure wings like those of Mercury, dealer to the gods. His dream was to go to Amsterdam, get covered in tattoos, and become a dealer.

As she ran, the girl thought, *Love binds us, that's why I'll never fall in love.* Casting bright glances, she hastily spotted nests in the soil and up in the trees, unable to distinguish medicinal from poisonous plants, measuring the bliss in their blossoms, pine needles sliding under her white satin shoes. The blue of the sea hit her at eye level from the other side of the island, a dark, deep blue. She hated the sea, the deep water. Every hour she had to spend on the yacht with her mother she pledged her existence to the salty air. He was still running after her, panting. From the corner of her eye she glimpsed his hair come undone. She slowed down momentarily at the sight of his loose brown locks, which he retied with a faded cloth, barely pausing.

They left the path, sidestepping the hill as if it were a mere backdrop. After a wide turn in the opposite direction, his palace came into view. It

was half in ruins. She regretted his wish to turn
it into a discothèque. She let him catch up so
they could take the final stretch together and
pass under the stone archway abreast. There was
no light in her gaze as she pursed her lips, jumping over a half-burnt mattress. She was scared
of fire, scared even of a plastic lighter's flame.
Sun shone through the holes in the roof. The di-
lapidated old tanning factory was all arches and
vaulted windows built from glimmering brown-
ish rock. The girl murmured, "What time does
it rain rocks?"

She ran ahead of him again, stepping on . . .
fish, little fish, fish in cans opening with rings . . .
empty sardine tins. "There's one more cham-
ber," he shouted with effort, in between gasping breaths. She passed him, jumping first over
the interior window's ledge. She landed five feet
away, avoiding a pair of panties and some other
trivial traces of life around a small gas stove. In
this second room, the water reservoir stopped
her in her tracks. A solitary flower with five rosy
trunks floated within the green foam. It reigned

like an all-powerful reproductive organ, ready to deliver a new dawn to its dominion. "It's alive," she shouted, both in disgust and in secret adoration. "Everything is alive," he shrugged his shoulders, raised as he was with his grand-mother's perception of the world. "Ah, here's what I was looking for," the girl said decidedly, as she drew an oblong miniature reliquary from her silver backpack. He could almost see black-clad women milling about with garters tight over their knees, all exuding the same perfume, women with inexplicable expressions bowing over the plastic flowers and the names engraved on marble tombs.

Her box contained rice and five clay toes of a human foot. "I molded and fired them," she told him; "once I win at the Olympics, I might study sculpture and make statues for the roofs of very tall buildings to be admired from airplanes." She gently closed the box again and threw it into the reservoir, where it was instantly gobbled up. With the sound of the last *glug*, he was reminded of his grandmother's sorcery. She wasn't simply a seamstress, she was a witch, best in the village for lifting curses and fanatical about TV competitions. She had already won three steam irons, three tangible proofs of the absence/presence of meaning in life. The girl kept staring at where the box had sunk in the green froth, and it seemed to him that her spell was cast strong. He heard her whisper, "My height's the problem, I want to be six feet, like you." He stopped himself from smiling, unable to imagine it. "I hope you win; I think you've got to become a runner—you were born to be." "Hmph!" she responded sarcastically, nailing him in the eye with a superior look, instantly deflating his attraction for her. He had always preferred losers. Well, not exactly; he weighed it and clarified it in his mind. He preferred the cursed because they have played with fire.

"I'm Axana," she turned and suddenly introduced herself. "It mcans 'stranger' in an Ionian dialect." Speechless, he watched her open the backpack again as she took out an elaborately embroidered cloth as big as a sheet and spread it over the wild grass. Its flowery patterns resembled suns. "It's a suzani," she explained. Each sun shone strongly and systematically over its world of wonders. The girl lay down, shutting her eyes tight. She took off her snug black blouse, an ornate, tattooed black eagle by her left breast. He lay down next to her. She unbuttoned her pants without opening her eyes . . . for a moment she bit her lip in a pained grimace. *I must, I must, it'll make me taller,* she thought, motionless until it was all over. Then she sprang up, emptying him onto her now-useless magic carpet, leaping out into the sun. At the sound of her loud exhalation, he ran to the window. He saw her, a petite ghost hanging in the air, sharp hair, pointed teeth, eyes like black slits, doing the highest flip, landing by the entranceway stairs, instantly taking off. She had disappeared past the curve in the road when he emerged, dizzy, into the sunlight, strolling downhill to the little bay, entering the sea to wash off her blood.

* * *

He was thirsty. It took him almost three-quarters of an hour under the midday sun to walk to the top of the village. When his grandmother saw him enter the backyard, she yelped with joy, hugging him, telling him to hoist her up in his arms. She had won a blue motor scooter on TV and it was to be delivered to them by Saturday at the latest. Yes, yes, he kept assuring her, he was very happy indeed. He gulped three glasses of cold water and went to sleep inside the old cool walls. Late in the afternoon, his grandmother tried to wake him with coffee and some homemade grape preserve in heavy syrup. In the end she pulled out the big guns, beginning to sing that childhood lullaby that always gave him the creeps:

> Far in the dark, deserted woods
> I dug my grave, to rest my head
> My black grave will burst in flame
> Setting the trees and flowers ablaze.

Night had fallen when he set out on the road for his father's café. The village kids were jumping over fires, celebrating the day of Saint John the Beheaded.[1] His cousin's friend had told him that in Athens they were planning to revive this long-forgotten festivity, burning televisions and cars.

He descended the trail among the pines. From above he saw that the girl's yacht had left. Though he was excited about the scooter, he didn't know why he felt so hollow under the red, heavy-metal moon.

Versions of
Persephone

As I watch the sunset through the window-pane the words select me: *vast, vulnerable, cracked, explosion, teardrop,* and an indefinite future.

The vulnerable room is outlined by mosquito netting. Axana is on time for her rendezvous with the explosion. Now she is running, laid out in a bed and closed in by netting. With her right ankle and heel bandaged, she soars from one beach to the next above the pine trees, Mercury's azure wings at her feet. But her inner determination to be an Olympic champion at twenty is shattered.

The actual room is vast, the bed placed in a corner. She's careful not to disturb the mesh folds with her breathing, so the shadows lurking at the corners—shooting her with a fanatical glance every so often—do not come any closer. They despise her, yet they take good care of her; this she cannot comprehend. Only the black guard who brings her food speaks in a friendly manner. There is a stateliness in his gestures, and he's clearly in need of a leopard-skin hat. The food is always the same: yogurt with oil and mint leaves, strips of unleavened bread, thin as shoelaces, and almonds with honey. He sits at the foot of the bed until she's drunk her tea, which softens the pain. Once her meal is over she hurriedly closes her eyes, shutting out his red tongue and the play of shadows against the netting. Among half-broken chairs, stacks of hardbound books, and cracked mirrors, the distorted mechanisms in their throats speak unknown tongues. The one she likes, probably their leader, often stands silently over her bed. He is pale, as if he's never been exposed to the sun. His brown hair, almost down to his shoulders, reminds her of the coffee-shop boy. The net opens on to the bathroom, and she dreads supporting herself along the walls on the way there. There is a hole in the ground, Turkish-style, no bathtub. She wets napkins, splashes water, and washes over the small sink. She gets used to the filth, the penumbra, the sourish taste of the low artificial light. The sole window in the basement is always shut. She misses the fresh air. Slowly, slowly, she gets accustomed to this too, accustomed to the language of losers.

Axana lives in captivity for an unspecified stretch of time. Does she remember it rightly or wrongly? After the operation on her heel, the Jordanian anesthesiologist and the Persian surgeon had slapped her back to her senses. In what she now considers her own private apartment in Hades, there is a platter on the nightstand with dusty pomegranates and an unlit clay lantern with $OP\Omega$ inscribed on the bottom.[1] The black guard sets the tea down next to it. At the foot of her bed a TV set doesn't get any channels, only varying shades of unnerving rain. With her eyes shut, she dreams of running. At sixteen she has the looks of a twelve-year-old boy, with very short black hair and broad shoulders. In her dream she's gliding on air, jotting down the names of unknown plants, varieties of the underworld untouched by her white satin shoes. As the dream turns nightmarish, she opens the filthy windowpane, the tightly wedged basement shutters. A tall mountain suddenly fills her mind's eye, casting its shadow all the way down to her bandaged leg. Snatched up in a tornado, she is transported to a flowering meadow, and the next moment she feels herself being lifted high onto a speeding golden chariot: she can see the horses' steaming nostrils and their rear flanks, the coachman hugging her from behind with frozen fingers, engulfing her in his cloak with a single gesture, just as the earth opens to swallow them up. The scream is her own . . . the scene . . . another abduction of Persephone by Pluto.

Axana awakes soaking wet from the moist heat. The one she likes stands above her. Just as their glances cross, she gets the feeling that he likes her too, because of her twelve-year-old-boy looks. He retreats and mingles with the other shadows, smiling as if he recognized her, as if they've got their whole lives ahead of them. Again she shuts her eyes tight in an effort to run back toward the midday sun. She would like to get at the origin of her haste. The time in captivity passes like a sickness. The air that was her element is scant and heavy. Her mother occasionally comes to mind in the form of a pillar of ice. More often, she thinks of her father. She murmurs, stubbornly at first, then with unexpected faith, "My father is a carpet merchant in Mercures' city. He has a thousand faces. He is an arms dealer, a trader of souls. He's an Albanian mafioso from the town of Argyrokastro, and only I know the true color of his eyes— the particular shade of cemetery cypress trees." She remembers their last encounter over two years ago, those ten days they spent together in a hotel on Marjeh Square in Damascus. She remembers him trying to convince her to take off her blouse. A Chinese man disguised as an Arab visited each afternoon to give her a tattoo identical to her father's: a black eagle, its wings spread, its eyes blue, so close to her left breast that she blushed. Her father, despite the price on his head, teasingly swore on the first watermelon he had stolen that this eagle could save her life one day. More Avenging God than human, he spoke to her of the 327 souls he and his gang had judged and condemned to death. Now that her body is no longer an airborne palace she remembers him in anger, so much anger that for an instant she feels strong again. Yet she cannot fathom how she could have arrived at a sprint the very moment of the explosion in front of the Vassilis Sofias Avenue flower shops, ending up lame. Again she can smell the burning steel, the burning flesh, her ears ringing. The majestic black was the one who grabbed her from the site of the explosion, holding her up like a shield. A real giant, whose head seemed to reach the second story of the French Embassy. Her foot hurt more than the passage of time itself as he fled through an underground arcade, carrying her on his back. Catching the smell of the fracture from within her body, she had fainted.

The pain keeps her in the basement. Not the handcuffs, since her palm is just narrow enough to squeeze through. *They're keeping me tied up because they still believe I am capable of escaping,* she thinks in a flash of her old willpower. Then again, she forgets herself in the language of losers. *I'm lucky I never woke up sobbing in this basement.* She isn't in any rush to find out if the damage to her foot is permanent. The black guard said that the blow had dislodged a tiny sliver of bone from her heel.

"You got rid of your weak spot." She lets him keep talking. Every time he comes, as soon as he sits down, he asks her what day of the week it is. Her response is routine: "Half past twelve, Thursday afternoon," the time and place of the explosion branded in her mind. Only once did she venture to ask him a question, so she could learn where he was from.

"I'm the descendant of a Yoruba king who didn't have much magical *àṣẹ*. What's important is where I'm headed, and how I make my way among those who consider me a stranger and a threat. I studied theology, and it was the Christians who taught me to love my enemies. That's why I'll take them with me when my time comes." He is well spoken, deliberate, making hardly any mistakes.

"Is that why you brought me here after the explosion?" But he goes on: "I'm on a quest for my own idea of time, which is cyclical. Each explosion is an escape from linear, Western time . . . Back when we were children we made plans to save the world, to save the beautiful scents from the Christians' destructive rage in the name of an indefinite future. Fear of death draws them to demolish entire mountains. We all lost a plant, a lake, or a mountain we cherished." She had never regarded death with fear. "My god is Mercury, the guide to the underworld," she whispers, but he doesn't pay attention. Is that why he brought her to this basement? Out of blind hate? For a while she has been holding back an urge to go to the bathroom, but now she has to get up. Her ankle seems even more swollen, and each movement is a fallen acrobat's nightmare.

As she washes over the bathroom's dirty sink, naked from the waist up, she sees — or feels — the door sliding open. Holding her breath, she keeps completely still. His long hair hides half his face. When he lowers his eyes to her breasts, his expression changes. The mask is cracking, and she can see something beyond a love for destruction in his stare.

"So this is why you're my girl," he says, touching the tattoo. Suddenly, the explosion-masters stop their coming and going. The curtains are drawn as everyone gathers around her, and she shows the eagle to thirty-two pairs of eyes. Her father, Viviano Varga, aka Viva, is their leader. He's the one who has trained them, who supplies them with weapons, explosives, and forged papers so that they can work as painters, plumbers, even pimps, she's sure of it. Her body becomes an airborne palace again in the brief moment that the black guard cautiously lifts her high over his shoulders. Now they're setting up a huge feast in the basement, and even the brown dog that sometimes slept by her bed does a number on tiptoe.

That is how her captivity comes to an end. They will take her out blindfolded to an unfamiliar square whose name she overhears: Prescription Square. They place her on a bench, but the one she likes whispers in her ear before leaving, "Nothing to be said right now, but the dog knows the way." Axana could have stayed there forever. The bench is in a church courtyard. Behind stained-glass windows, candle flames pray. She stumbles on garbage, trips on gas canisters and bent spoons. Large cardboard boxes are stuck to the dark facades of deserted houses. As she passes by a ground-level room with lit lanterns surrounding a statue of a black-and-red ox, she hears the difference in her step. The pain shortens her gait. She arrives at Prescription Square and stops, breathless, in front of an old man perched atop a makeshift canvas throne on wheels.

"You in a hurry? Scared they might mug you? Why not mug you and your foreign smell?" *I smell unwashed,* she thinks. They've gathered round her mockingly. Someone with a red rag tied around his forehead dives at her shoulders and pushes her.

"Where am I?"

"This is Prescription Square. People with deep pains come to have their prescriptions filled. If you don't like it, you'd better pray you disappear." She is nearly pushed under the wheels of a passing taxi. Axana crawls inside and gives her mother's address, hating the cold luxury that awaits her. *I don't know where home is,* she thinks.

She endures the months after the second operation like a potted plant on a balcony. The doctor told her that she'd never run again, that she was lucky she hadn't lost her leg, lucky it would only drag a trifle . . . confirming her thought, confirming that she has no more reason to live. Now what?

Motionless on the wicker armchair in the garden, listening to helicopters flying toward the center of Athens, she follows the change in seasons. The distant explosions are all the more frequent, but nobody offers an explanation. She caresses the head of the brown dog that appears each afternoon; Axana has named him Halfpastdoom. In this interval of immobility, she judges and condemns her father to death.

Fall comes to an end, a chill spreads in the garden, and on the first cold night she gets dressed and silently sneaks out. Halfpastdoom knows his name by now, happily sniffing at the houses and their large gardens. Each time she calls him he stops short and waits for her, wagging his tail. They walk a long time, perhaps two, even three hours, her foot hurting, the cold mounting, the darkness deepening. After they pass the train tracks, they find themselves once again at Prescription Square. People dressed in rags have lit fires in barrels, tossing around half-eaten sandwiches.

"Hey, this cig's on me," one of them yells to her.

"Beware, they'll steal your eyes, snatch your eyelashes," a one-eyed man screams, swinging a white cane above his head. Halfpastdoom jumps with joy at someone taking off his helmet. His brown hair has grown longer, falling past his shoulders now.

"We must avoid the checkpoints," says the one she likes, as the three of them get on his motorbike. She fumbles at the gun in his jacket pocket.

"I want you to take me to my father," she shouts in his ear. Just where the city should be ending, an unknown city begins sprawling out. Its windows are dark, boarded up, condemned. An orange glow tears at the sky, the echoes of distant street fighting chasing after them. But once again, Axana has a purpose, and this renders her fearless. Maneuvering, they pass a half-wrecked bridge, crossing over a stream littered with trash. The earth trembles from a muffled explosion, and she turns to see the gaping hole of cement and steel behind them.

"Promise you'll always be my girl, no matter what," he shouts back to her. "Say it." The sweet warmth of his body from beneath his clothes startles her. She hugs him tighter, a solitary teardrop running down her cheek.

The End of Matter

On the small dock below Vaporia, the affluent sea-front quarter in Hermoupolis, I sat drying after a brief but sweet swim. I fixed my towel on the blue plastic straps of the chair. I drank my beer, marveling at the foam, making out the remnants of some sea celebration. A ship was leaving port, and the waves it raised reached as far as here, crowning the rocks. Suddenly two palms closed over my eyes.

"C'mon, Dimitri, I know it's you."

"Tell me, who'd you want it to be?"

Dimitri let go of me and brought himself a chair. *Alkis isn't anything anymore,* I repeated to myself . . . *neither menace nor promise, nor the Eurydice I wish I could bear back from Hades. He's just the shadow at my left rib, still there after so many years. Insubstantial but persisting, a nightmarish treasure.*

"What's with the attitude?" asked Dimitri.

"Whoever liberates my desires—over him shall I blow the colorful smoke of disaster."

Dimitri got up, dipped one foot in the sea, and turned to me with a happy glance.

"How about it . . ."

"Too bored." He dove in the water, and I just sat there, drinking beer.

The young man passed by me, barefoot. He stood a few feet away and began undressing. He threw his button-down shirt and pants on the worn cement dock. Underneath he wore pink boxers with gray stripes. He was lanky, the perfect young runner's body, like Alkis. He turned and looked at me, the hour and sky belonging to him, even if his heels lacked wings. From a parallel life I noticed his eyes, somehow deep in their sockets, hardly reminiscent of a winged god who might bear a soul aloft. In his eyes I glimpsed the dark life of the deep. They brought to mind the eyes of drowned men, just before the fish go at them. His beauty troubled me, confusing thoughts of eternity with a desire near pain in my stomach. I watched him dive, ready to follow.

But instead of plunging, searching for his embrace in the water, I turned my chair so as not to face him. I smoked a cigarette, lost in the gulf, a seagull bringing me back to the present every so often. Behind me the houses were built on steep cliffs, a few of them nearly hanging over the water. Seaside houses, some like petrified amphibians, others with small, well-hidden gardens clinging to their sides. Again I started thinking of Alkis. For three years I beseeched every force, visible or invisible, to bring him back. Wind, water, earth, and fire I had begged, I had prayed before pliers, screwdrivers, moldy yogurts . . . every clock I faced I implored to give me that moment back, allowing his body to flood my senses. I felt as if I could see him again, playing with the water, salty eyelashes blinking out the light. Palms covered my eyes for the second time. Small palms, a child's hands.

"I'd like to be together with Adora on her magic horse and beat Katra in that videogame.

What about you?" Jason's sweet voice whispered in my ear.

"I like Hermoupolis. When we go for evening walks, it feels like such an airy city, a city with winged ceilings." He pulled away his hands and sat in Dimitri's chair.

"Where would you like to be?"

"In a cape called the End of Matter."

"Will you show it to me on the map?"

"It's not like the Cape of Good Hope; it exists only on secret maps. The all-powerful winds that blow there snatch away your wishes, and in the end you lose your memory, you lose it all, even your name."

"What is matter?" he asked me, and I pinched his arm. He let out a small yelp and laughed.

"Dimitri is coming, ask him to explain what matter is."

Behind Dimitri, the young man emerged from the sea. I stood up. He stopped shaking the water from his hair and stared at me as I dressed in front of him slowly. I gathered my things. Jason had worn the plastic water wings, and Dimitri was drying his ears with the towel's edge.

"Two beers and I'm done. Off to sleep," I told them, getting up to leave.

Brown Dog in
November

I could always tell where the dark side lies, even as a fair little boy in shorts, back when I used to run countless circles around myself. By the time I grew up, the gray and the black had lodged in my mind's right side. There images of the women I have loved jumble in confusion as they struggle to the surface. At one point I had loved them all, as long as they enjoyed me tying them up with the threat of a tormenting caress. Who knows what else they had in mind, perhaps even a violent death. The repetition was my little game that made them fade away.

What is a small room inside a big room? A sad room, like an underground reservoir with barely visible walls moistened by the lost years gone by. That's where I used to live — and from one day to the next, years went by. Numerous dark corridors led to unknown beds and to those naked bodies. They enjoyed it, their entire bodies trembling, writhing at times. I liked it too, though their faces meant nothing to me. I chose them to be indifferent so their sharp breaths wouldn't catch me by surprise, so I could bind their elbows extra tight. Their pores exuded a warmth almost visible in the half-light. My sad little room was set apart from those dim spaces where the telltale smell of bodily pleasure hung, but I always knew I would return to it. And so I extended the ritual, giving all I had to their tight white bellies.

The conditions of submission and a contract of provisional but absolute surrender made me so well behaved and so gentle, my haste to forget them unforgiving. In cafés, at bookshops, at the pharmacy, even in taxicabs, I heard them call my name, "Nino," that slightly girlish nickname I used to introduce myself. Instantly I knew they belonged to those stale, drunken, early-morning hours, back when without much protest I had them all to myself, and though I could have killed them I granted them life. "Nino," I heard them call, sore with myself for not remembering them. I never lay down with a single one more than twice because I knew that afterward they would seem unforgivable. I proceeded like this calmly and sure-footedly until one night, passing by our old house, I was caught once again in Eleni's orbit.

Winter had mounted an assault in the previous twenty-four hours, chasing the leaves from the trees. The sky had turned white, and it dripped wet snow over buildings still steaming from the endless heat waves of summer. This change in temperature coincided with daylight savings time, this sudden succession of short days and those first frozen nights ruining my good disposition. Eleni was still a safe distance from my life, but I could feel her streaming toward me, encircling me, transfixing me with the brightness of an obsessive thought. She was closing in on me — a blinding fountain about to suck me up. The image came to me — I too would soon find myself tied up for the first time in the strands of her electric storm.

What is white? The sky is white with dense white clouds. Who, really, is Eleni? The *el* in her name stands for an ancient ellipsis known to all.

That's why I'm scared of her. Yet she is the only one capable of transforming the mechanical repetitions of my little game into holy madness and my little passions into true love, loosening my bonds so she may be redeemed herself.

My nightly jaunts thinned out. More than anything else it was the dogs I met on the street that lingered in my memory, it was them I kept talking to . . . I saw her/saw her, I kept seeing some of their sweet faces until I cut up my medications overnight, so I could focus all my attention on Eleni's traces.

There are many things I do not recall. When did the dream with the lions start repeating itself, the lions sprawled out wall to wall? They were the wardens of my prison. And my sleep among them, my only safety. Could they belong to those nameless naked women who pledged their submission to me with such ease, waiting to devour me the moment I woke? Around the time this dream surfaced a hushed voice began whispering all the more persistently. Was it Eleni's voice whispering about the dangers of those red manicured nails? It whispered, nearly commanding me to walk in the sun, to avoid the dark side. In the beginning it was entertaining to converse with her in hushed tones as we strolled. I asked her opinion on small matters, as if we were bound by an agreement of sincerity and detachment.

As soon as I was positive it was Eleni's voice I began to wonder: Was she hiding from me, disguised as a married housewife with a child? Living her life half-asleep just like me, her breasts spilling onto the sheets round as full moons, sesame seeds strewn on the bed?

In an effort not to think constantly of her I began digging at those stone walls with the sharp railings of my memory, searching for something irrelevant to her curves, her body, or her voice. I paused momentarily on an image: as a child I had seen a horse struggling among cars, its hooves slipping on the asphalt. That horse was white. Late at night when I would return home, having escaped those red manicured nails, a dog would lie sleeping in the middle of the road, blocking the entrance to my apartment building. That dog was black.

One evening, heading downtown to find an open newsstand, I realized I wasn't sure about having seen that white horse after all. But I was certain there wasn't a dog in the whole city that didn't dream of shredding Eleni's silk stockings, rubbing its muzzle on the white skin between her thigh and loose panties. The dog turned over, exposing the scant fur on its belly. Eleni, invisible, was stroking him and feigning ignorance. Surely she knew the stray dog's life I was bound to lead until she domesticated me once more with her voice. Quietly, the dog kept dreaming of us. I threw a stone at him and he shivered with the fear of a shouted *Scram* and eternal hunger. Then he recognized me—Eleni and I had adopted him on a walk during our honeymoon, bringing him home with us on the ferry. It was on the evening we had taken that walk to the gorge, the flanks of the gully filled with rhododendrons in bloom that shaded her perfect lips and the sky in the same color. That night her breasts were the most wondrous thing I had ever kissed. More lovely than the full moon. Just like a game, I wanted to tie her to the railings of the old bronze bed in the rental house. Jokingly, I pretended I wanted to tie her tight so I could then take my time choking her, making sure she would never escape me. She slipped away and stopped laughing, her body instantly distant. Could she really have been scared of me? She was coughing, trying to catch her breath, glaring at my hands. I set her free and she turned her back to me. Soon, she seemed to have drifted to sleep. Listening to the exhausted breaths, I knew that in her sleep she had already abandoned me, already sweeping endless monastery corridors with an improvised broom of thorns. Outside by the cluster of cypresses, a pack howled at the moon, hungry for her breasts. With her eyes shut, Eleni smiled, and the dogs hushed at once. I calmed down too, as there would be no shadows left between us, no bad memories. When I woke up, Eleni had left. A bewildering succession of summers have

since passed me by, stuffed with pills they told
me to take for the anxiety, for the sleep problems and the tremors in my hands. Equinoxes
have slipped away; so have lonely holidays in
winter and spring. The divorce was filed in winter, around then I think, in the abyss of the late
nineties.

Not all nights were the same. In the great
cold spells of the November full moon, when
everyone was sharing the same inexplicable
dream of being sentenced to hard labor in the
salt mines of uninhabited planets, I would walk
for hours gazing up from one church dome to
the next, pacing their courtyards in search of
a little earth under my feet. I was trying hard
to pledge myself to God, but Eleni kept breaking my train of thought . . . when she was in a
good mood, I inhaled her deeply through both
my nose and mouth—then she was my girl—
whenever she left a crack of faith open for me.
Whenever I couldn't sleep I would pace through
dark alleys with stout dozing dogs. The ember of
my cigarette led the way, and somehow I would

always end up in front of the house where Eleni and I used to live. Our old apartment was lit up. From the gossip going around at the corner store, I discovered that the young woman now lived there, the one I kept running into with a child in her arms. She kept avoiding my gaze but her aura was identical to Eleni's. Hidden behind the angelica bushes, I waited on the chance that she would come down again, hoping to hear her voice. Black dogs/white dogs/brown dogs were sleeping in front of the building door.

The young woman with the baby in her arms walks on the sunny sidewalk, speaking to it softly. I follow her from the shady side until I see her enter the building. Soon her husband will be returning in his gray car. At night, when the apartment lights flick on, hidden again in the angelicas, I will speak my mind loud and clear . . . *You think you escaped me now that you've re-married, just because you have a husband and child? You think you can all go on a trip to a rhododendron-filled gorge in that gray car of yours with its roof rack? Stretch-*

ing out on the sunny side, warming up, lying down and embracing like snakes in the grass? You, smiling— you wear your spit for lipstick so well—smiling: a slit in your coral lips because you don't know that I can shred your world to pieces with my teeth—if your little girl has your looks—if she yells at me, commanding me in your voice, "Don't bark Nino! Don't you dare bark!"

The Uninhabited
Body

The bus hacks and sputters. Hacking and sputtering it invents its route from the start, divining the tumble of trim houses, their displacement by bleak apartment blocks. In the future they'll eat on top of one another, sleep on top of one another, dying a hospital death and instead of a sleepless wake the final solitude of the uninhabited body in the funeral parlor fridge.

But now we still have the old bus with the ticket collector, and our heroine is very young, though not untouched. It's just that she despises the haste of those who touch her. Here on the bus seat, however, her eyes fixed out the window as she feels the pressure on her thigh, a wave of warmness washes over her. They share a secret understanding. They must never look at each other. *I will be in love with you for two more stops.* He knows her hours to and from English class. They inhale together, and together they empty their lungs, utterly slow and secret. Mainly secret from the others. Soon, a tiny shared tremor. Out of the corner of her eye she can only see a patch of the brown corduroy pants. *I'm crazy about you, my corduroy fabric, what an effort it takes to part.* She rises with difficulty, turning her face away the whole while, presses the button, and gets off.

Her first love awaits her at the stop, his blue eyes calm; he seizes her in his embrace, and as he lifts her off the ground there is haste in his body. *No comparison with my corduroy fabric,* she thinks. Then she takes him by the arm and they begin to walk, talk, laugh while her mind slowly recovers from the numbness.

Rain in Arabia Petraea

Could be a drowned woman's suicide
note
Could be the scribblings of an opium
eater

I remember the moment our gazes met in the Amman bazaar. Among so many dark eyes I singled his out, blue-gray, a bit blurred by images of another time. He was standing in front of a fluttering column wrapped to the top in colored scarves. He too appeared to be a foreigner, like me. My husband and I passed by the city's only drunk, who sputtered as he held an empty bottle in his left hand, "My name is Fouad, I've lived four years in Germany." From the bottle's mouth, his Germany spilled out. I wore my wedding ring on my right hand. Ten years of marriage slipped through, wasted. The stranger kept staring at me with a smoldering cigarette in his mouth. He had long brown hair and a slightly crooked nose pointing westward, his mouth gentle but insatiable — well drawn yet unfaithful. I wouldn't mind being a bit unfaithful, I said to myself as Timon squeezed my hand. The stranger's lighter wouldn't work, but my flame ran straight toward him and when he blew smoke back to me I could see the cloud that would bring rain to Arabia Petraea that night.[1]

*   *   *

His gaze arrests me in the shell of some other era. The sun drops below the horizon the very moment he transfixes me with his eyes. I feel transient and drowsy as the light fades over roof-tops where all the city's scrap metal lies rusting. *Allah* resounds from the minarets, and I see the column, his hand, his body trembling. His eyes roll. He's heaped up two paces away, a nearly visible demon sucking his breath.

When at last he stops writhing like an anthro-pomorphic fish, foam is streaming down his chin, a bloody thread reaching the cobbled pavement. Suddenly Timon is out of sight; I look around, but the crowds have swallowed him. Reluctant for a moment, I want to turn back, to find my-self at home with the television switched on and muted, a freshly baked cake on the table to gain some time — the hardest part is when I know he's expecting me to take off my clothes.

I realize I am following a mourner's path. I hail the first passing taxi, and instead of return-ing to our hotel I make a deal to travel through the night on a four-hour journey to the ancient city of Petra. I dream of dazzling funeral monuments as the black sky begins to spill darkness over the car. Lights glimmer here and there. The driver and I keep silent as we pass them and continue forward.

I recall only the public baths at the entrance to the small town. I remember the empty reception desk at Abdullah and Ali's inn. A feast has just fizzled out. Drawn to the dining room by a flickering fire I see the remnants of a party, all the plates piled with leftover pilaf and grilled meats. White flowers lie withered on the floor. In front of the fire, the stranger from the Amman bazaar stands alone. A bruise is visible on his forehead. He opens a paper bag, producing a bottle of red wine.

At first I want to dash away again, but a small human-like creature donning a hood with tiny bells starts pulling me by the sleeve. A second brimming cup appears in the air, as in a fairy tale. We drink slowly, looking into each other's eyes. Years could pass like this in an opium dream. Not the way they were dragging on with Timon, I don't want to remember that.

I'm almost sure the brothers, Abdullah and Ali, came to our table fingering their shiny black beards, teasingly murmuring something about an upstairs room.

I struggle to keep my eyes open. A dim memory comes back to me, the dim image of a large room overcrowded with single beds, only one of them made for us.

Inside the room a deathly cold emanates from the black-and-white tiles. We take off our shoes, we lie down, while outside the skies burst into rain. We are wrapped tightly in the only quilt, our backs touching. Just when I expect him to turn around and hold me, the sound of a woodwind arrives through the window. A melody so sweet, so sorrowful, as if played by someone contemplating suicide.

In the absolute darkness I hear the stranger's voice for the first time, in English, a sort of sing-song: "Tonight is the longest night of the year."

Tonight the witches fly over the necropolis, I

can feel them groping at crevasses shut tight on all other nights.

"Lydia," I hear his voice again, and I could swear he pronounced it softly, like a Greek.

"Lydia, I have been searching for you a long time both on earth and in the clouds. Traveling to Jordan, I knew for sure I'd find you again tonight by this necropolis . . . At the bazaar, the demon inside me still sought revenge. And yet in Haiti I had to kill you, as I myself had to die, so that I could offer you an absolute love.

"When I transported you by boat from Port-au-Prince to the witch's island across the bay, she did more than wake you from your coma forcing you to drink that pale blue liquid, she inhabited you. That's why nothing mattered to you anymore, nothing but your blind mirror. That's why the vulture would come and settle on your shoulder, both of you nibbling at cactus fruits that painted your lips and his beak bright red . . .

"I killed the vulture with a silver arrow, the witch with a golden one. I was consumed by your presence just as much as by your absence. Nature herself laughed at my misfortune. Now I know, you are Fire and I am Water. Now the mysteries of the world belong to us. Allow me to extinguish you, and make me evaporate. Only then in the sea's immeasurable depths, where earth's lava flows, liquid trees will ignite for us, flaming flowers. Each year on the winter solstice, our grief will be reborn as passion."

I awoke soaking wet. It was dawn, the room empty. No sooner had I pulled off the quilt than a thin layer of ice covered my body. The faucet turned itself on. I ran to the reception desk, water rushing down the stairs behind me. Abdullah and Ali had vanished. I walked out on the muddy terrain, the rising sun drenching my body, everything evaporating. Then for a moment I remembered you, my poor Timon, wrapped tightly in your raincoat, a white speck blacked out by the crowd. I recalled your restless eyes. You'll always be angry that I slipped away. But there is no going back. Forgive me.

Stormy Verbs

Reflected in the bathroom mirror among the wooden hangers and damp towels, Verbia's features seemed about to crack. Lately he had sensed that something from her past had shattered her. *She entered into my life messed up,* he thought, and he felt guilty for having wanted to stick with that first impression. *From the moment I looked upon her,* he criticized himself, bringing the razor to his cheek again, *I wanted to capture her beauty. I was deluded into feeling I could have been her creator.* Verbia, remote again, smiled politely and absentmindedly—it was this very expression that had started worrying him lately, her eyes so dull . . . *What, Verbia?* he wanted to ask, an obvious rhyme passing through his head, *What a shame, am I to blame, I see you growing sadder* . . . He said nothing. As she kept softly brushing her hair, A. Brandas cut himself. He saw the shock in her eyes at the sight of the blood. When their gazes met in the mirror, Verbia shot up electrified and cut the corner off a tissue, sticking it on the small wound. It looked like a snowflake had fallen on his face, white all around with a red target in the middle. Though he had mastered the art of setting limits in his professional life, he felt himself losing his grasp . . . Outside, from the country road, the sound of a car engine was heard gasping. A pickup truck was hauling a young gray horse in its flatbed, tied by the neck.

"I will take you to feel the force of a river hidden behind a mountain, the wrath of a river that first divides in two, arriving at the sea weakened in many separate streams. Rocks big and flat like frozen mattresses have rolled down its riverbed. But first I want you to see a gigantic tree that I once loved, with a love tempered by respect," said Verbia, casting him a sidelong glance. The gold flecks in her gray eyes were on fire, like gems caught in the sun, unearthed after centuries buried underground.

She was driving up a steep hill on a desolate road all potholes filled with chunky gravel and thick, unbroken mud. It looked as if no car had passed by these parts for a long while now. Even Castello Rosso, the crown jewel of the coastal town of Karystos, was now below them, and they continued their ascent. A storm was hanging from the sky, the landscape filled with sharp rocks that sprouted up like teeth scattered across the whole hillside. A war waged by giants seemed to have ravaged the landscape that weighed heavily on them, oppressing them. Brandas tried in vain to imagine spring visiting these parts with its flower buds and chirping birds. The very soul of the grim land felt unforgiving. He wished they would head back to a café by the beach, to read their own newspapers. Every turn in the road enhanced his anxiety over what kind of revelation she had in store for him. *Verbia, forget it,* he wanted to say, *we may live in some kind of vitrine, but believe me, it's better than the dark basements I have visited as a psychiatrist. I'm tired of fumbling in the fog, tired of breaking rocks. Because whatever was buried alive must first be brought back to the light, and then, if you manage to set aside the fear or the shame to deal with it, only then will you come to terms with yourself. Verbia, that's exactly what I fell in*

love with you for, your special way of being hermetically
shut and your fragile but unbreakable balance.

Verbia hit the brakes, jolting out of the car,
and he got out too. His first impression was that
his ears were buzzing from the altitude, until he
guessed the presence of the river. She ran ahead,
stopping only to get rid of her shoes. Motionless
for an instant in the frosty air, she was sweat-
ing, though she wore nothing but a thin woolen
dress—a red dress; he had never seen that color
on her before. Brandas pulled up his collar to
protect his ears from the cold and the river's wild
dialect. *Verbia, why did we come up here?* he stopped
himself from asking, but he kept thinking worriedly: *up till now she was still my little doll and I'm*
about to see her inner workings. She pointed at the
old ruin. "It's the chapel of the Forty Saints. The
forty martyrs condemned to die of cold. Shep-
herds in the area call it Winter's chapel, while
others, because of the ancient column you will
see inside, believe that it was an ancient sanctu-
ary for Dionysus many years ago, where mae-
nads briefly took shelter before wandering on

the slopes in search of live prey. Rumor also has it that winter begins here each year, descending and spreading over the Western Hemisphere."

An opening gaped in the remnants of a wall, and the whole church seemed to sway. He followed her inside, a carved marble column holding the last standing arch in place. The wooden prayer bench had fallen, blocking the door. There were no icons; just the remains of some mismatched seat cushions and a cracked oil lamp on the floor. *A single sigh suffices to cave the roof in,* Brandas thought; the river and its vibrations have shifted the foundations, possibly even rotated them, hence the narrow window behind the shrine seemed to face northward now.[1] Outside, at the back end of Winter's chapel—or, as he would later think, the chapel of a wasted Spring—a giant sycamore tree shot up, the one she must have been referring to earlier, he assumed. Verbia emerged from the ruins too, but she passed right by the tree, climbing upward among the wild ferns, ahead of him once again, a persistent spirit drawing her forward.

She ran uphill as if her naked feet could read the ground in Braille. Though it was not in his nature to follow others, he hastened his step. The harshness of the landscape awoke a kind of rage within him for all the years he had spent listening patiently to the problems of others. She stopped short and changed direction. A half-wrecked sheep shed stood at their left, and he got closer to take a look through the opening. Two large, rusted oil drums had been placed there to serve as chairs. In the middle of the room was a make-shift table, and on top of it a blue vase brimming with dead flowers. In the forsaken landscape, this spooked him the most, as it seemed to summon the presence of a being, sensitive yet able to converse with the rocks and the almighty river. He imagined a primal creature, a sightless creature unable to shed its tears, wearing burning coals in its empty sockets. Verbia arrived first at the middle of a small plateau and froze there, statuesque. He approached her slowly, searching the ground for bloody traces of her feet. But the cold moss kept her secret. The river, a true deity, bellowed invisible in the depths of the gorge. Brandas was in awe. Verbia turned her head in his direction, her hair disheveled, her features distorted, sharper, forged by the river's merciless verbs. An unknown woman stood there inhabiting her clothes, resisting him from within that dark red dress. Her body gained strength from the elements of nature, the frothing water, the trembling earth, the unbearable weight of the sky. A black dog bounded out of nowhere, and Verbia turned and started running straight at it. *They'll devour each other,* thought Brandas — *a maenad and a wild dog. A reluctant spectator once again, I'll watch a worthy battle.* With a leap the dog landed at her feet, instantly turning back, the rocks closing in behind it. As a yellow slice of sun appeared, painting the opposite hillside in a bitter shade of lemon, Verbia kneeled. Brandas took a few steps toward her, trying to quiet his gasping breath. The river was still invisible, the tall rushes blocking the view to the bottom of the gorge. He called her name softly, in an invocation to remind her of what she was when he had fallen in love with her: candid, ethereal, and cryptic. Feeling his presence, she started moving her lips. Was she talking to him? Sleep talking? She gestured, urgently motioning him away and then rose slowly, stretching out, her body now a bow, now an arrow that soared above the rushes at the gorge's edge. Brandas could have sworn he saw her taking two–three steps over the void before a cry loosed itself from within her. Only then did she fall and vanish. He would always remember the horrible thought that struck him at that moment—this nameless woman had returned to the abyss that gave birth to her.

Still a stranger to the fact, Brandas approached in slow motion and bent down to look. The foaming river below rushed over rocks as big as frozen mattresses. On one of them, Verbia's body seemed to have shrunk to an almost fetal size. He could barely grasp how his life had already changed . . . Verbia's broken body chased him back to the car. Only when he got hold of the steering wheel did he notice his entire body trembling.

*   *   *

Brandas wished he could have summarized
the following days with a single phrase: *I saw
a funeral and followed it*. But not even the narrator's mastery of the story can overcome the
nightmare that went on for ten whole days . . .
The return to the gorge with the rescue crew
. . . the night in the holding cell . . . the wait
for the coroner, who took his time arriving from
Athens. He addressed him only for a moment,
doctor to doctor, confirming that Verbia's body
had shrunk indeed: at the moment of impact the
femoral bones had jutted far up into her chest.
On the second night, Brandas moved to the
fifth floor of a hotel by the waterfront. They had
politely asked him not to leave Karystos, and he
was under the impression that he was being followed. The whole time his comings and goings
to the precinct continued, a strong wind blew,
and it seemed to him that it scattered a sleeping
powder. He was constantly tired. He was aware
that such a reaction of denial wasn't unusual, yet
his eyelids kept closing. He got no rest though,

since at the threshold of sleep, Verbia kept appearing before him carefree and happy, just as when they had first met. *I fell in love with her hidden flame,* he thought, *but I took care not to burn my fingers.* He would get out of bed, draw a chair up by the balcony door, and watch the sea till daybreak. But no door could keep out the indiscreet gazes. When the chief of the Karystos police department, who had personally taken on the investigation, asked him about their last night at the stone guest house, he realized how much the postmortem had revealed to them. He withheld the fact that she had been begging him to save her. Verbia had woken from a nightmare, speaking unintelligibly about a swarm of insects creeping over her. Ensnaring him wildly in her embrace, she stuttered in the language of the senses as if his sperm were indispensable to her survival.

The cold air jostled chairs and tables over the town square's marble tiles toward the sea. Shunning curious gazes, he was in a rush to get back up to his room and hide. He was only sure of one thing: when this process was over, he would close up his medical practice and begin a long journey—dust from distant continents under his feet—that was all he wanted.

Late at night he would walk up and down the long, long jetty. As he observed the piled boulders supporting it, he resented all kinds of rocks. How little he knew about Verbia; he was unaware that she had grown up in Karystos, that her family grave was here in a small seaside cemetery resembling the deck of a ship. The blinking beacon of the lighthouse reminded him of a poem he had read when he was young and idealistic, its title "Dying in the Singular."

It was his last night in Karystos. He had gone out again and was walking along the jetty when he heard rapid steps approaching on high heels. The woman wore an oversized man's coat and had covered her hair with a flowery scarf. He pulled away in surprise as she introduced herself, touching his arm. Under other circumstances, her face could have been charming, he thought.

"You are . . . ," she hesitated, "Verbia's husband. I was her best friend in high school. I've been watching you pace here at night from my window, but it just now crossed my mind that Verbia might not have told you. Do you have any idea what memories that place held for her?"

"Not exactly, she told me she wanted to show me the power . . . of a river . . . perhaps, in the end, her own."

The woman's eyes welled with tears.

"I could not imagine she was still so unhappy after twenty years."

Now Brandas wants to know. *Fiat lux,* he wishes and secretly commands.

"It seems that Verbia never forgave herself for flinching, for pulling her hand away from him at the last moment, two steps from the gorge. They had a suicide pact."

Now that he was burning to know, the woman had to pause? Gaining time, delaying her return from the past to the present?

"Maybe they discovered they were siblings. That's what some people were hinting at here in our town. They shared that same dazzling beauty. The only time they let me see her, before they sent her off to finish school in Athens, Verbia was terrified and inconsolable. "I got scared, scared of him," she kept telling me, "And now I cannot keep on living." Brandas's mind halts. He hears words, phrases—he only registers the last one. "I want you to know that I will always light a candle for her soul."

He looks at the woman as she walks away, dragging old ghosts behind her. He shifts his gaze toward the dark sea. The reflection of the lighthouse beam startles him, reversing the title of that old poem. "Verbia," he whispers, "now I know your secret. In your shortcut to oblivion, you are not alone."

The Silkworm's
Address

Once upon a time there were holy trees, holy stones, and a snake, the holiest of them all. My first memory is quite simple though: that of a little rug at his apartment door, surely left behind by a previous tenant. That's where every New Year stumbles. That's usually how it happens. The evening arrives, a moment swelling from my longing to return, to pass through that front door's keyhole and cracks, retrieving my twenty-three years of age and my love for T.

His eyes conjured up the funerary stelae of Alexandrian times. Those dark eyes with the whites shining, often resting on me, had the power to transfix me, his eyebrows bringing to mind a royal eagle's wings spread open in flight. And T. himself seemed to possess a hidden ability to fly. Air was his element, and with the wind I still welcome him. That winter it hadn't surprised me that our feet were hardly touching the ground as we walked together. I guess I shouldn't have been surprised that he flew away and vanished . . .

I fell in love with him on the 8th of a long gone November, a day in which all things lost, everything invisible, is celebrated by the ephemeral world, as it was revealed to me years later. Outside our window the wind blew strong, setting free its dogs, the zephyr, the sirocco, the ostria, and the tramontane. It blew so hard I thought the gusts would blow right through me, and I struggled for breath.

The bell was broken, and I knocked lightly on the door. When I found myself sitting awkwardly at the edge of the bed, I clearly remembered a woman's voice on the radio, singing, seeking revenge against her lover, who had stripped her of all joy. I never heard that song again, but T.'s voice returns each New Year's Eve, whispering in my ear, "Remember when a day wouldn't pass without rapture?" I wish I could remember less from that house, where no red light had been flickering, indicating a way out, warning me of an emergency landing.

It was a strange house, floating above the world. Though the bathroom stood opposite the front door, it might as well have been flung far into an empty lot, since our bodies were hardly human and only tangible in bed. There were two bedrooms, one quite dark, opening on to an air-shaft, and the other overly bright, just like the living room. Both looked out on the community pool, Zappeion Park, and Lycabettus hill. The furniture and objects were of an obsolete elegance, the semicircular sofa clad in yellow velvet, a coffee table inlaid with mother-of-pearl arabesques and on top of it an ostrich egg. Numbers—or were they dates?—sometimes formed in the crimson rug, running and hiding in the weaving. On the floor our only pet, a sharp sword from the Philippines, rubbed at our feet.

Testing the omnipotence of thought, we would turn off the heaters when it got really cold, our foreheads burning. On rainy nights I opened the windows, inviting thundering oracles, calling in the lightning to turn us to ash before the summer light washed over us. Winter swept quickly through those rooms, invisible silkworms wrapping us in their feverish cocoons. As if we were fasting, we'd both lost over twenty pounds in five months.

The weather had warmed by the time we arrived on the island. Without the fog surrounding us, without his steaming breath, I hardly recognized him. I remember thinking that on our last walk beside the sea, as our steps in the sand strained for the first time. "Do you believe in God?" he asked me all of a sudden, echoing the cedars on the beach, the pebbles and the sea creatures—seals, whales, and all the tiny clams. "I believe in the invisible," I replied, "and I feel awe for the boundaries keeping me apart from these cedars, these pebbles, all the sea creatures."

We caught the last boat and returned to Athens that same evening. Late at night a strong hot wind came up; T. had fallen into a deep silence a long time ago. I was slowly descending into the well of sleep when I heard his voice.

"In this we are not alike. Though I am lacking in faith I aspire to the grace of God." Drowsily, between half-closed eyelids, I saw the luster in his eyes for the last time. I felt him rise from the bed and heard him going out on the balcony. I awoke at dawn to a silent house. The front door was locked from the inside, but I still searched the house and balcony, every single drawer, averting my eyes from the gravel at the bottom of the airshaft. I kept searching for three years, slowly acknowledging that what we've loved is never lost, even if it returns back to earth. Sometimes on the morning of New Year's Day his voice still dares me, "Don't waste away your time with a slow death." Hastily, I take up pen and paper to fill the gaping mouth of Time with words.

Dogwise

To Angie and Libby

Last June I could feel the impulse of an ancestral dragon stumbling over blazing-hot tar. Heavy heat had set in by May, and as happens under extraordinary circumstances, some have visions while others become visionaries . . . so one day, at midafternoon, I sensed a very beautiful woman hidden in the body of a dog down by Exarchia Square. I realized it as soon as I spotted the black-and-white border collie, its ears so agile, so sharp. But it was mostly the eyes, sensitive and moving, of exquisite beauty, all the more stirring in their lack of self-confidence. A dapper young man sat a few tables away, holding her tied on a short red leash. When he saw me staring, obviously under her spell, he turned to me with a shy and conspiratorial smile. I approached. As I stood petting her velvet muzzle, he confessed to his extraordinary love affair . . . Zennia had appeared to him suddenly, hungered and dirty, without a collar; she the most beautiful dog either of us had ever laid eyes on. The rest of his words were

swallowed by the heat and a beggar's monotonous soliciting complaint. I vaguely remember
him saying that no harm should ever come to
Zennia, how she was all he cared about, adding
in a whisper that such devotion was nearly a sin.
As I was fondling her white neck a sudden shiver
ran through me. Zennia was planting seeds of
her past in my thoughts . . . When she was twelve
years old, twelve of the Supervisors' adolescent
sons had bathed her in their sperm, but the one
who had bought her in the end, the one who had
tormented her all night in his embrace, was old
Zig, the galaxy's most outrageous millionaire.
For the next eight years, each 40th of the month,
he offered her rape as a spectacle to his guests of
honor, screaming, "Planets for sale, delusions to
trade, but only Zennia for keeps."

*Those who control us present everything as a spec-
tacle,* I thought. My hand jerked from her muzzle,
dripping with sweat. I turned hurriedly back to
my table, but jumbled human words kept find-
ing their way into my brain—was it some kind of
forbidden love between Zennia and her oppres-

sors' son Zig-We the Just? "Do not betray me," her beautiful eyes now pleaded from a distance; "my mother, my own mother, sold me for thirty years of youth. Do not betray my secret. I have ways of knowing that old Zig is seriously ill, that he has used up all his time deposits. They feed him with a broth of his servants' tears, yet his teeth keep falling out. Soon they will be scattering his ashes over Deimos and Phobos, the twin satellites of Mars."

June again this year. Cool temperatures. Light rains wash off a red dust arriving from Africa. Nothing surprises me anymore, and I expect the worst. The wind cracks jokes, but the city is bitter.

I hadn't gone out for coffee in a long while, and somehow I ended up back in Exarchia. I wouldn't have noticed him if it weren't for his insistent stare, the way he was playing with the red leash in his hands. I got up and walked over to him once more. He was unshaven and poorly dressed, his eyes evasive.

"What happened? Where's Zennia?"

"Well," he drew a long breath. "Zennia just disappeared," he said in a thin voice. "She vanished two months and four days ago. I awoke in the middle of the night from a torpid sleep. Music was drifting in from down the road, curling with the ambiguous seductiveness of a snake. Zennia was gone, the kitchen door leading to the roof ajar. Now her little plate, her water bowl, and this leash are the only proof that she passed through my life . . . I've lost my job, and they'll be evicting me soon, but I still wander about at night calling her name. Tell me, please, wasn't she an exceptional creature?"

"Oh yes, she was very special, enchanted and enchanting, maybe even much more than that. Her beauty was such that it wasn't only hers to enjoy. You should be content you cared for her." A drizzle began tap dancing merrily on the café's awning over our heads. The heavens were about to open up, our feet soon slipping in filthy mud. I addressed her silently. *Oh Zennia, I hope you are happy with your lover, and that together you may change your world with justice. A while had passed without my giving a thought to your innocent beauty. You shone like the critical drop of blood that can unsettle the balance of centuries, even of millennia. You shone like the drop of blood that will soon spill here too.*

Althea's Prophecy

In the time of the Great Disaster, construction of the milky dome over the old volcanic crater had been hurriedly completed. This was back when chain explosions had condemned the human species to live under the earth's surface for over eighty years. In those sealed basements, along with anticipation for the Exit, hung a dread of hostile masses who would activate their own magnetic fields on May 24 of 2129.

Louis Achelous was eleven years old.[1] His grandfather, Francis Nile, would turn sixty in a year. His expiration date and euthanasia ceremony were coming up. Following an injection of immeasurable happiness, his body, clad in white, would be launched onto the surface of earth. So he was in a great hurry to teach his grandson how to pick the antimatter locks. While others attended scheduled recreational activities, the two of them would sneak inside Level A air ducts. There in the narrow, concave hallways, they glimpsed the historic center of Athens projected on the tunnel walls for the Superiors and the Supervisors. Louis liked Heroes Square best because he could just make out a spotted black-and-white cat in one corner.

"Look, a real cat!" his grandfather had said to him when he noticed her for the first time. "Nothing to do with those simulated fairy-cats in your reading room. She has a silken coat and purrs when you pet her." Louis did not understand. He only knew the constant purr of the air ducts, and whispered question after question.

"What does *silken* mean? Why do they meow instead of talk? Do cats laugh?"

"Animals do not laugh," said his grandfather gravely.

"And why do we have to laugh when they teach us Jokes? What a relief it would be to laugh freely!"

"Why is it called Heroes Square?" Louis asked that night, as the skaith tried yet again to rip the dome apart with their beaks, echoing like blasts of wind above the dome. It was at that moment that Francis Nile attempted to explain self-denial to his grandson. But little Achelous was getting confused; he wanted to know, his parents who had absconded through the air ducts only to die after wandering briefly on the poisoned surface of earth—were they heroes?

"No." For the first time his grandfather decided to reveal the truth. "They were desperate to escape. For this, they had been condemned to lifelong underwater imprisonment. You should have faith in real cats, in true plants that give off beautiful smells . . . but above all, you must believe in and await the day of the Great Exit."

They felt their eyelids grow heavy. It was the first time they had strayed this far, and the imposed sleep was getting the better of them. The grandfather, aghast, urged Louis through the air duct, worrying about how many things he had forgotten to teach the boy. Barely a child, he had entered the dome as a specialized worker in Mass 1. He still dreamt of the tree turned to ash before his eyes—he had made an oath to that tree, and this was the reason he took these risks in the artificial night. Under their shared blanket at last, he whispered to Louis with numb lips.

"You must believe that the Ancient Prophecy of 1048 will be realized . . . back in the time of the Althea eclipse it was revealed to Velhudius the Great Astronomer that Evil will be forever defeated after the Great Exit. You must hope, hope that you too . . ."

Next to him in the common cot, Louis was already fast asleep. Old Nile barely had time to register the first spasm, their bodies jerking rhythmically as the red glow kept piercing the walls of their underground cell. Something inside him snapped, his tree dissolving into dark refractions . . . what is a tree? Their thoughts had already disintegrated, their mutation into dummies destined for slave work in Under-Mass 2 complete.

Grace

Many are the undercurrents that run between my memory and the memory of the world . . . Back in the distant froth of childhood, where new seedlings buzzed in the young belly of spring, even the threat of chains was sweet because they'd be made of fragrances—lilacs, four o'clocks, Arabian jasmine. Winter was a tunnel, always finite, from which we'd emerge. We could even climb to the bell tower if we wished.

It was early spring; I was ten when my father brought her to our townhouse in the Athenian neighborhood of Nea Smirni. He had picked her up from a nearby park bench, teary and bruised. At first, she didn't say a word. She sipped a coffee, swallowing it with difficulty. Her voice wouldn't come out because her throat was all knotted up. The second coffee she drained with pleasure. Looking back on it now, I'd say she did it with a lightness almost inappropriate to her condition. When my mother served her a glass of warm milk, she suddenly looked at all three of us one by one with great care, and whispered in a soft voice that nothing terrible had happened to her, because her firefighter, her Panagiotis, loved her deep down. My parents became furious. After declaring a Cold War on one another ever since I could remember them, they were shocked by this version of love. Anyway, the decision was taken almost immediately: we'd keep Grace home with us, she'd help out with the housekeeping, have a small wage, and my father would make sure to admonish Panagiotis.

Grace was twenty-three years old, but she didn't look more than sixteen. We left her in the bathroom to wash up, and when she came out, wrapped in a white towel, searching through the closet with my mother for clean clothes—who knows how that deeply buried red dress with the taffeta tail caught her eye, the dress an aunt in America had sent. She donned it immediately. The first night at our house dressed in red like that, with her long black hair, with her shining black eyes though one was bruised, I thought she'd start dancing a dance of fire, and every movement of her bony pelvis would spread the gleaming tail like a fan.

Next morning, in simple clothes, her hair tied back, the red dress all hers by now but hanging in the closet, she did everything with levity and joy, without a trace of haste. The first time Panagiotis drove by in the red firetruck and honked, Grace spilled into the road and my father invited him upstairs to the living room so the men could have a talk. Teary-eyed, Panagiotis didn't take long to give his word; he would never raise a hand again, he wasn't to blame either, he'd had such a nasty childhood, his dad having knifed his mom to death.

That year, the tunnel of winter ended particularly early. Easter, though, was late to come. And suddenly, on Holy Thursday, Grace announced to my mother that she'd take me to church to hear the Twelve Gospels. In the street, bells pleaded sweetly. In front of a garden with an illuminated fountain, between two of Judas's blossoming trees, she explained her plan to me. She wouldn't cast a spell, but make a binding pact: with each Gospel she would tie a knot in two belts, one hers and one Panagiotis's, fastening herself to his pajamas.

"That way we'll never separate and always love each other," she added. Her jaw seemed to be trembling. When the lights came on again after the Fifth Gospel, and as the nailing of the cross still resounded, I saw how her eyes had filled with tears. "You must believe and you must pray," she bent down and whispered to me. A gust passed through the three open gates, warmed by the candles, heavy with scents, caressing the icons. Then I shut my eyes tight and made a prayer.

"Oh wind, unruffle my mind, oh wind, rid me of this shiver, bring instead a joyful quiver."

A few days after Easter, Grace left our lives forever, running down the stairs of love not caring if she busted her knees. In her wake the house's temperature fell again. With my fingernail, I could trace a *No* onto invisible frozen windowpanes. She took the red dress and its rustling tail with her, and we learned from the neighbors that she was beaten all black and blue again. We wondered whether she'd left us without saying good-bye because she felt ashamed.

I saw her once more ten years later. It was Holy Week again. My parents didn't exist anymore, and I lived with someone I had sworn never to love. This path of mine was strewn with flowers and razor blades. The taxi driver had looked at me the wrong way from the start because it was close to noon and I was still wearing the previous night's long black dress. Arriving at a small street in the neighborhood of Kypseli, I discovered I had forgotten my wallet. His eyes lit like lightning, with hate but also with a hidden joy; "I want my money," he began to shout louder and louder as the crowd gathered. An ivory-faced young woman bent over and asked: "What does the girl owe?" Grace paid for the cab.

Back then, I was never coming, always leaving, and we only spoke for two seconds. She and Panagiotis had never broken up. After the kids were born, he'd calmed down; he was a good man now, going to church every Sunday. Yes, they had two daughters, little Flame and Maria of the wind. She kissed me and crossed me, and for one instant, as her cheek touched mine, it came to me to say, *You and your belief in miracles, ask your God to save me, drag me out of these cold murky waters, tear away these black bindings restraining me. Here where I find myself in a razor-sharp eternity, grant me one deep, free breath.* Tears welled up in her eyes. Her empathy didn't surprise me, that's how she was—always ready to lift the weight of the world. Her grace touched me for a moment and I felt the first sweet promise in the air. Without saying a thing, I left at a near-sprint, and it didn't matter at all that a world of cheap glimmers was swallowing us, separating us forever.

Zenaida Junona

A voice, monotonous at first, a sung obsession like a quiet threat, love sprung from the illuminated platform. The orchestra flew higher—pausing, awaiting her, and when the woman's voice burst forth, it seemed her breath was inexhaustible. I remember tripping the moment I laid eyes on her— the sprained ankle, the pain, and my near tumble—a near fall dedicated to her magnitude. The woman herself was miniature, half her face scarred with burns. From the intact side, flames seemed to sprout. Her black skin shone with sweat, mirroring the bright little red lanterns. Her armpits were drenched, her emerald dress stained with salt. She sang motionless—I would have fallen into her had K. not pulled me up and set me back on my feet with a steely grip. His cold fingers passed on a possessive message for the first time in so many years of exchanging roles and wardrobes. They brought us a carafe of their own kind of sangria, amberish-orange and thick with slices of unknown aromatic fruits.

The waitresses were svelte and tiny. We were the only whites in there.

I couldn't guess her age: fifty, sixty, maybe seventy. Her voice trickled an unknown feeling inside me that immediately took root and spread, mimicking my veins—a matching map of growing expectations. The woman was nearly a dwarf, with wide feet, open-toed shoes, and nails painted phosphorescent orange—like her lips. She moved her mouth almost imperceptibly, and the song spilling out in that unknown tongue could have sprung from the world's primordial well. Leaning her head to the left, she sang a song that seemed dictated by the first black slaves. Out of the corner of my eye I saw K. refilling my glass; I saw him dropping in that powder again. Ah! K. and his little potions. Something to put us to sleep, something to wake us up, to get us going, to bring us right back to where we started. I took the glass without taking my eyes off her. She held my gaze, and it seemed as if she smiled, as if a little flame on the

untouched part of her face had bowed to me—
could it be possible?—I emptied my glass into a
flowerpot and started drinking from the carafe.
Her ribcage hid reserves of gold and silver, sharp
gravel and water grinding in her mouth. I drank
without getting drunk, my mind growing clearer
with each strong sip, with each minute flying
by. She was suddenly short of breath, a small
cloud escaping from her nose. In a hoarse voice
she ended the program, and in this final song
a younger me recognized elements of a rumba.
The refrain was in Spanish and she repeated
it with her soul catching at her lips: "Beber lo
nuestro comer lo nuestro ahora sí, van a vivir
lo nuestro" (Drink like us, eat like us, yes, now
you will live like us), the same words repeated
mechanically by the big white parrots in the
courtyards of Justa Fé. She rose with her shoes
in hand and stepped heavily across the planks of
the floating platform, the seawater below ebb-
ing and flowing. As she passed by me I smelled
fire, I smelled burnt carnation. I turned to see

her opening a low door in the back of the joint, and just managed to glimpse the red walls swallowing her up.

"When's she up next?" I asked our young driver while K. was paying. For the first time, an abyss was gaping between me and K. Such a sudden abyss.

I was rarely resolute enough to refuse his little powders, to pour out the coffee, the tea, the fresh juices with his concoctions. And all I knew was how the one that resembled pink Himalayan salt set me up real good and sent me swiftly to sleep. But I had managed to learn the singer's name, Zenaida Junona. I must have whispered it in my sleep, and I'm sure K. heard it. That's why he kept me hostage with a weight on my eyelids— with that pink mist that curled all the way out to the seafront. Days had passed by the time he finally propped me on my feet and took me on a walk as the sun was setting.

"What do you see?" he kept asking. It was our old game, I CAN SEE IT, CAN YOU? But once again he was the one failing to see—a big game of hide-and-seek in the low clouds—and from the celestial thief's bag a trail of lights fell in his wake onto the sea's surface, changing the substance of the mist.

"What do you see?" He was asking insistently, a thinly veiled anger in his voice for the first time in nine years, I afraid of him for the very first time. Zenaida Junona—I kept invoking her name in secret, as a shimmering speckled cloak spread out to shroud a decommissioned ship at the other end of the bay. A strange ship, small and rusted.

"I like how the game is getting rougher now," I said to him as we stood in front of the small lighthouse on the jetty.

I was hoping for our young driver's bad cough to foreshadow him—hazy as it had all become, his cough announced him, materializing him. I was hoping for him to come and tell us when Zenaida Junona was to sing again . . . K. and I strolled along Justa Fé's three wondrous roads by the port, among yellow houses fitted with red shutters. Farther inland the colorful shanties sprang up, stuck together with spit. There, on those zigzagging roads, we kept running into corpulent dogs that came up to us and beckoned with human eyes.

"My dear sir," they would say, "dear lady from across the great water, can't you see we've been transfigured, please do something. Our pious mayor gives us a little food, there is plenty of water left and right, but we are hungry and thirsty for a different sustenance. Maybe if you took us into your bed, maybe if you loved us, something would finally spring forward in this arrested universe."

Life indeed seemed at a standstill in Justa Fé. All the action was around midnight; that's when they aired out their sheets, when smells wafted from the chimneys. As I think back on it, a succession of empty roads, closed shops, and small deserted cafés comes to mind. The food at the hotel buffet, where we had to serve ourselves, was an odd mixture of raw and cooked stuffs. I do not know whether this too is a trick of memory—all the dogs were brown, the parrots brilliant white, and all the cats a coarse-haired gray.

In any case I'm sure I saw and heard her sing once more on that same floating platform. I remember her wearing a red dress. K. got up provocatively and headed to the bar in the middle of her last song, at the very moment she was giving her life away along with her voice. Our driver then whispered in my ear that she lived on the decommissioned ship, that she had but one white teacup and a few packets of coffee and sugar, and rumor had it she slept in a solitary chair. She dedicated the last verse of the song to me, avoiding my gaze. I somehow grasped the meaning of the unknown words: *It doesn't matter how many battles we lose, for in the end we will win the war.* This time as she passed by she threw me the carnation she wore fixed to her décolleté, withered by her flame. It fell on my lap and in a deft magician's gesture I hid it under my skirt. Perhaps K. had crossed paths with her on his way back. He looked very pale, his inscrutable gaze troubling me.

A thirst tortured K. at night: for all the feelings he did not have, for all he could not see that I could. Anyway, that same evening my turn had come to throw some of that pink powder his way . . . I got up before the sun rose, and in the uncertain light I slipped my bathing suit on under a long dress. The sea of Justa Fé usually had a preternatural shade of green that I'd only seen in a painting of Breughel the Younger. That dawn— *madrugada* in Spanish, a word that brings to mind a morning execution—I was met with a yellow sea. The decommissioned ship was not too far away. If only I could shake my body awake I'd be able to swim across in a quarter of an hour. I wondered what promise that woman's voice could hold, wishing I could lay my head on her lap and be reborn. As soon as the lukewarm water reached my ankles, stories came to mind of electric clams whose favorite appetizer was human eyes—of sharp black coral that would close in, sealing you in an ornate coffin—and of other amorphous creatures preying with a burning desire to take up a feminine form, lurking, ready to rip out your hair by the roots, braiding it with seaweed. The moment the sun dawned, the sea became striped, yellow red green, the marine flag of an unknown state about to wrap me up for a sea burial. No one had prepared me for what happened when I took two more steps into the water . . . An invisible force grabbed me by the knees. Struggling in vain, I saw myself passing her ship with dizzying speed, ending up two miles away from the beach. Then, a standstill. Yet when I tried to swim back, the same dense, underwater force blocked my way. Only then did I remember reading about sea currents in shallow waters. To return to shore I would have to swim at a forty-five-degree angle. I just lay on my back, my body reluctant to fight, my life not worth the trouble, floating, hoping only for a quick end.

An hour must have passed when I felt something nibbling my thighs—small, nearly transparent fish were picking at me. That very moment, I heard someone call my name. It was an incredible spectacle: K. dressed in white, pedaling leisurely toward me on a water-bicycle . . . That is how K. saved my life, or granted it to me as a useless gift.

The next day he got me to the airport and we left, so drugged was I that in Madrid I remember being transported from one airplane to the next in a wheelchair.

Four months passed in Athens before I managed to recover. With a will of its own, my body reacted to whatever drink he brought me. It all mysteriously gushed from my mouth as soon as I shut the bathroom door behind me. That's how it happened. K. didn't realize it, but on one June afternoon, I was wide awake. It took me another week to recover my prowess as an escape artist and stitch my cloak of invisibility. Secretly, I made lists of all the things I could fit into my old canvas bag embroidered with birds by the Kuna Indians. I didn't go through the trouble of searching far away, renting an apartment just two streets farther up the hill, certain I would abandon it quickly, leaving the key in the front door. Insomnia succeeded fatigue. In the dark I often tried to imagine the look on K.'s face when he found my farewell note by the coffeepot, as he read the signature, Zenaida Junona, instead of my name.

Early one morning I ducked into a travel agency. I told the young man the name of the country, and when I specified the city, he winced, a door swinging shut in his eyes.

"Let's see," he stalled, his fingers sliding across the keyboard, a strong draft whipping paper and dust through the room. "Justa Fé," he announced, "was obliterated two months ago by a hurricane."

And now as the story ends, my life must begin. I must build it from scratch though I'm unfamiliar with the materials. First I think of fasting to cleanse my body, and then of cleaning the small apartment, washing the windows though the view is cold and unremarkable. I stand on the balcony scrubbing the windows when my own voice surprises me. I realize I'm singing aloud for the first time. A young couple stops under the balcony. I notice the girl—not only do I notice her, I feel her ready to fall to her knees. The boy, jealous and arrogant, pulls her by the arm. But she stands her ground, enthralled by my voice, the voice of Zenaida Junona springing from the world's primordial well.

The End of
the Show

Late at night I sit in the courtyard observing one of nature's tiny detestable drills buzzing at the outer walls of the house. It targets them, trying to dig a hole the way all wasps do. Then it makes one big mistake; it pauses on the screen door. With measured movements, I enter the house and spray it from inside. Though I soak it, it doesn't fall. I step out and sit down again, observing it. Noiselessly now, it fights to reach the bright bulb. For each step gained, two or three are lost. Creature of the sun, how come it strayed here at this late hour? Now it struggles to reach the light before it dies. Obviously it will fail, I can see that. But the very moment I expect it to fall so I can scoop it up with a broom, my secret human cruelty buzzing to a peak, it spreads its wings, flying high, darkness swallowing the end of the show.

Translator's Notes

DOWNTOWN ATHENS

1. In 480 B.C.E., the defeat of the Persian fleet at Athenian hands was decisive for the future of the region: had they won, the Persians—not the Ancient Greeks—might have exercised their influence on the rest of the world.
2. See Revelation 21; the original city mentioned is Jerusalem.

THE SUZANI AND THE SCOOTER

1. Saint John the Baptist, whose feast day is celebrated in Greece on August 29.

VERSIONS OF PERSEPHONE

1. "*OPΩ*," pronounced "ō-ró" in English, is the verb "see" in Ancient Greek.

RAIN IN ARABIA PETRAEA

1. Arabia Petraea was a Roman frontier province in the time of the empire, whose capital was Petra.

STORMY VERBS

1. According to tradition in the Greek Orthodox Church, a shrine's window must always face east toward the birth of the light.

ALTHEA'S PROPHECY

1. The Achelous River, one of the longest rivers in Greece, is also known in Greek mythology for its patron deity of the same name.

MARIA MITSORA was born in 1946 in Athens. She attended the University of Paris–Sorbonne and Vincennes before returning to Greece in 1976 after the fall of the military dictatorship. A key figure of the underground literary movement in the late 1970s, she has published four novels, a novella, and two short story collections. She writes regularly for magazines.

JACOB MOE translates from Modern Greek and Brazilian Portuguese, and is a recipient of a PEN/Heim Translation Fund Grant from PEN American Center. He is also co-founder and director of the Syros International Film Festival, and a producer of radio programs in Greek, Portuguese, and English.